DARK USURPER

When Alison returns to the house where
she ha   nes,
at Abe   DATE DUE   nds,
Keith Heseltine does not share her belief
that it is possible to be content with
memories of the past. But because she had
been very hurt when the beautiful, ruthless
Geralda had stolen her boyfriend Toby,
Alison is in no mood to accept Keith's
advice, even though she had to admit that
her feelings for him appeared to be different
from those she had had in her childhood. It
is only when Geralda appears once more,
now intent upon Keith, that Alison realizes
that his advice to her had indeed been wise.

S0-CIG-065

spent many happy childhood ti

DARK USURPER

Henrietta Reid

ATLANTIC LARGE PRINT
Chivers Press, Bath, England.
Curley Publishing, Inc.,
South Yarmouth, Mass., USA.

Library of Congress Cataloging-in-Publication Data

Reid, Henrietta.
  Dark usurper / Henrietta Reid.
    p.   cm.—(Atlantic large print)
  ISBN 0–7927–0260–3 (lg. print)
  1. Large type books.   I. Title.
[PR6068.E437D37   1990]
823′.914—dc20   90–31591
                                                          CIP

British Library Cataloguing in Publication Data

Reid, Henrietta
  Dark usurper.
  I. Title
  823′.914

  ISBN 0–7451–9812–0
  ISBN 0–7451–9824–4 pbk

This Large Print edition is published by Chivers Press, England, and
Curley Publishing, Inc, U.S.A. 1990

Published by arrangement with Harlequin Enterprises B.V.

U.K. Hardback ISBN 0 7451 9812 0
U.K. Softback ISBN 0 7451 9824 4
U.S.A. Softback ISBN 0 7927 0260 3

© Henrietta Reid 1972

Photoset, printed and bound in Great Britain by
REDWOOD PRESS LIMITED, Melksham, Wiltshire

All the characters in this book have no existence outside the imagination of the Author, and have no relation whatsoever to anyone bearing the same name or names. They are not even distantly inspired by any individual known or unknown to the Author, and all the incidents are pure invention.

DARK USURPER

CHAPTER ONE

As Alison studied her reflection critically in the dressing-table mirror, then a little dubiously applied more eyeshadow, she heard Geralda, sprawled across her bed, give a throaty chuckle. 'Am I overdoing it?' she asked uncertainly, watching her friend's expression reflected in the mirror.

Geralda Conrad pulled her slim figure upright and wound her arms about her knees. How beautiful Geralda was, Alison thought a little wistfully: her trouser suit of emerald-green silk complemented her strange amber-coloured hair and the green, almond-shaped eyes that now watched her with amusement. Or were they faintly derisive? Did she only imagine this? Alison thought uncomfortably. After all, Geralda Conrad was so exquisitely groomed, so much the poised woman-of-the world. And Alison herself—well, she had always realized she was no beauty and probably the only reason that Geralda had befriended her in the first place was because she had a flair for knowing just what would sell like the proverbial hot cakes in Geralda's boutique, The Gilt Cabinet.

'Well, you *are* overdoing it, aren't you?' Geralda vouchsafed at last. 'I mean, with your colouring, it's fatal to lay on too much

1

eye-shadow.'

Alison nodded resignedly. 'Yes, I know. It makes me look too much made-up; that's the worst of having so little colour.'

Geralda yawned. 'Let's say you're not the theatrical type; some people can get away with loads of eyeshadow and lipstick, but it just doesn't happen to be right for you.'

'No, I expect I'd better stick to pale rose lipsticks and lavender water.' Alison replied a little wryly as she stood up.

'But it's not like you to be fussy about your appearance,' Geralda said. 'There must be something special on tonight to make you so particular.'

A faint pink touched Alison's cheeks. 'Yes, I'm meeting Toby,' she conceded, 'and I've the feeling he's going to pop the question.'

Geralda swung towards the bedside table and with deliberation selected a cigarette, slowly lit it, and blew out a stream of smoke. Keeping her head averted, she said, 'Tell me, Alison, are you in love with Toby? Really in love, I mean? I want to know the truth.'

Alison gazed at her in surprise. 'But I've already told you I think he's going to propose. Is that not an answer? One doesn't marry a man without being in love—to a certain extent.'

Geralda nodded. 'Oh, I agree you're in love with him 'to a certain extent', but frankly, from what I've seen of you and Toby, I shouldn't say it's one of the great romances of all time. Somehow I get the distinct impression that—oh, let's be blunt—that you're taking him to escape the boutique.'

Alison gazed at her friend, wide-eyed and a little shocked. 'Oh, but I love working at The Gilt Cabinet,' she exclaimed. 'I enjoy every minute of it. If it hadn't been for you, I'd have been stuck at some ghastly desk, typing for a grumpy old employer.'

'All the same, naturally you don't look forward to an indefinite future of being chief buyer and trouble-shooter and general dogsbody at the boutique. Apart from that, I'm well aware I'm no sweet-tempered indulgent employer. I fly off the handle at the drop of a hat. And you're so utterly different in temperament! I expect at times you long to chuck it up.'

It was true, of course! Geralda's temper was inclined to be sudden and unpredictable. But was that really the reason why she was seriously considering marriage with Toby Benson? Alison asked herself. Yet Geralda's words made her feel faintly uncomfortable. It was true that with Toby she didn't have that sense of overwhelming rightness she had always expected to experience when she met the man who was to be her future husband. There was no encompassing, overwhelming emotion to sweep away all doubts and hesitations. No, with Toby she had kept her feet very firmly on the ground: she looked forward to marriage with a certain dispassion.

But then Toby himnself was not particularly romantic. He was an acute businessman who had managed through application and hard work to make for himself a position of respect and comparative affluence in the small rather ingrown town of Market Hanboury. But already it was only too easy to imagine his smooth, bland face overlaid with middle-aged pomposity. His unctuous, rather pedantic manner too gave him an air of premature age. Yet Toby had no vices, would make an ideal husband and was considered quite a catch in Hanboury. In fact she rather gloried in the envious glances cast at her when she was in his company.

She gazed frowningly ahead as she considered Geralda's words. 'Now you're making me begin to question my motives,' she said, a little resentfully. Her marriage to Toby, which had seemed straightforward and inevitable, now began to raise problems.

'But don't you think it's a sensible thing to question motives? I mean, now at this stage?' Geralda pursued. 'What's the point of waiting until you're floating down the aisle to wonder if you're making a mess of your life? Now is the time to give a bit of thought to your future, before things go too far.'

'What do you mean, "go too far"?' Alison demanded sharply.

4

Geralda shrugged and studied the tip of her cigarette. 'Oh, simply that when you get to the stage of buying the ring, it makes it a great deal more difficult to back out—that is, I mean, if you wanted to.'

'But of course I don't want to 'back out', as you call it!' To her dismay Alison realized her voice was shrill and defensive. 'Why on earth should I do such a thing?'

She studied her friend in frowning puzzlement. It wasn't like Geralda to take such an engrossing interest in her affairs. Once outside the door of The Gilt Cabinet her life and Geralda's sharply diverged. Geralda knew a host of highly sophisticated people: she moved in a world where her beauty and rather acid turn of wit was an immediate entrée. And her time, when she wasn't actually in the boutique, was spent in London. Whereas Alison kept pretty much to the interests of the local community.

'And where are you meeting your heart-throb tonight?' Geralda asked.

Alison opened a drawer, took out a handkerchief and put it in her handbag, glad that Geralda had at last abandoned her psychological probing. 'Oh, I'm meeting him at the boutique. I want to go through some of the stock, so I'll set off early and give myself time before he turns up.'

'My goodness, you are a glutton for work, aren't you?' Geralda yawned and stretched her lithe form on the bed. 'I can't imagine myself going back after a hard day's work.'

Alison was aware that Geralda considered her devotion to duty as merely a confirmation of her stodgy and provincial outlook.

'Oh, I don't mind. Actually I rather enjoy it,' Alison said, defensively. 'It's the kind of work I've always longed to do. I love the variety of colours and materials and textures—and then there's the fact that I've chosen them myself, and that they're actually popular. Somehow—'

She stopped as she saw the look of utter boredom on Geralda's classic features.

'Rather you than me. I don't pretend to appreciate your aesthetic satisfaction. However, the clothes sell like hot cakes, and that's all that counts as far as I'm concerned. Anyway, it's time I was dressing. I'm going to the theatre with Mark and he likes me to look as glamorous as possible. But then that's the way men are: you're supposed to be dressed up to the nines with all your warpaint on, whether you feel up to it or not.'

She got to her feet and again Alison got the uncomfortable feeling that in her employer's eyes she was a non entity; a pale insipid shadow in the background of Geralda's life.

Could this consciousness of her inferiority to Geralda possibly be the reason why she had let her friendship with Toby develop along its inevitable lines, Alison wondered, as she

6

walked along the street towards the boutique. She felt a resurgence of resentment that her motives should be questioned—tonight of all nights—when she expected Toby to give her his ring.

He had brought up the subject at their last meeting. His rather unctuous voice had said playfully, 'You'll have to tell me, Alison, which are your favourite stones, or else I'll probably make an awful bloomer. You women are so superstitious; opals are for sorrow; pearls are for tears; emeralds are bad luck. I suppose we'll have to stick to diamonds.'

She had hesitated. Toby's voice had held its usual patronising tone when he spoke of the vagaries of women. He would probably consider her own choice completely unsuitable.

'My favourite stones are aquamarines. I love the cool, clear colour, like frozen water from a grotto in Capri.'

Toby had stopped and gazed at her with something like horror. 'Aquamarines! But they're not really good stones. People would think I'd scrimped on the ring. I mean, you must consider my position in Market Hanboury,' he had added, portentously. 'Oh, no, my dear girl, it's completely out of the question. No, let's make it diamonds. It's conventional, I agree, and possibly doesn't satisfy that rather romantic streak you

7

have—which, by the way, my dear, you'll have to try to get rid of. It's inclined to disconcert people when you come out with such things. 'Water frozen from a grotto in Capri' indeed!' He had suddenly squeezed her close, chuckling as though indulging a rather precocious child.

After that he had not brought up the subject again. Had her answer disappointed and discouraged him, she wondered, perhaps emphasised to him the difference in their temperaments? Toby was a cautious person, slow to come to a decision, especially about anything that would affect his career. Was he perhaps reconsidering, pausing judiciously before committing himself?

Yet somehow the thought didn't affect her as it might have done before her conversation with Geralda. Things had been spoiled by Geralda's penetrating questions, for doubts had been raised on her side too, troublesome, niggling doubts that were, however, shaken off as she reached the boutique, the front of which was cunningly formed to simulate the glided façade of an eighteenth-century cabinet.

She felt in her bag for the key, opened the door, and stood for a moment on the soft, thick carpet, surveying the racks of shimmering clothes; the blues and turquoises and gold; the glow of burnt orange and ultra-marine; the wild whirl of colour and design that made the little boutique one of the most successful enterprises in Market Hanboury.

She crossed the carpet and caught a faint waft of Geralda's favourite perfume, a dark, spicy scent as sophisticated as its owner. Geralda had insisted that their customers would associate it with The Gilt Cabinet and now during business hours a stick of it was always burned in a holder in the corner of the shop. This was the only way in which Geralda had imposed her will, for she was acute enough to realize that in Alison she had found someone who had an uncanny flair for clothes and in her capable hands she had left the complete buying and stocking of the enterprise.

But now the sight gave Alison no pleasure. In fact, she felt a shadow of unease as she surveyed her handiwork. Could Geralda be right? Could her motives in encouraging Toby Benson have been nothing more than a subconscious wish that the future should hold something more than the boutique? The fear that she might one day become like the acid, gimlet-eyed woman, Miss Pringle, who kept the florist shop next door and was continually talking about her 'disappointment'. Would she too find herself disappointed and maybe begin to resemble the proprietress of The Rose Bowl? Alison wondered as she walked down the shop absently running her hands along the gleaming rails, her feet silent on the thick dove-grey carpet. She glanced at her watch. Toby would be meeting her shortly. It was time she got her priorities right and decided exactly what she desired from life.

It was at this moment she realized she was not alone and, with a little startled exclamation, turned to find Miss Pringle standing in the doorway. 'Oh, it's you, Miss Pringle,' she said with relief.

Miss Pringle nodded, her sharp angular face looking excited and at the same time sly. 'I didn't mean to frighten you, I'm sure, Miss Lennox, but I saw the light on and I guessed it would be you, for Miss Conrad doesn't take the same interest in the business, does she? And anyway, I wanted to have a word with you in private. I was working late, doing the bouquets for a wedding. The bride-to-be is dreadfully fussy; she wants mauve sweet peas and crimson roses—such a horrible colour scheme! But she insists. But then brides are inclined to be fussy, aren't they? After all, a girl's wedding day is the most wonderful in her life—or so they say,' she smirked sourly.

Alison waited, puzzled. Why had Miss Pringle bothered to come in? she wondered. Toby would be arriving soon and the time she wished to devote to her own problems was being frittered away in this inane conversation.

'Oh yes, indeed, you've no idea how

10

troublesome some of the customers can be,' Miss Pringle pursued. 'Very high and mighty and full of themselves. Just because they're getting married they treat poor little me like dirt. Not that I mind, for I had my own chance—though it didn't work out: his mother was against it and he didn't stand up to her. But perhaps it was for the best! I often think that many of those girls are making a dreadful mistake. So few of them know what their boy-friends are really like. There's no doubt there's a lot of truth in the old saying, 'Marry in haste and repent at leisure'.'

Alison gazed at her perplexedly. What on earth was Miss Pringle talking about?

The proprietress of The Rose Bowl advanced a little further into the shop, the brilliant lights glittering on her high coiffure. 'You don't mind if I say something very confidential, do you, Miss Lennox? You won't take offence?'

'No, I suppose not,' Alison replied uncomfortably, feeling a growing inexplicable uneasiness. There was a satisfied glitter in Miss Pringle's pale eyes as she began, 'They say it's always the wife who's the last to know, but there are a lot of girls who are shutting their eyes to the fact that their boy-friends are doublecrossing them. Not that I mean that you knew,' she added hastily. 'No, it's someone looking on—like me—who spots these things. You know,

11

when I realized what was going on, I couldn't believe my eyes. Mr Benson's not so handsome and—well—Geralda Conrad is such a very sophisticated sort of person; the type who would set her sights on someone very wealthy and wildly attractive.'

Alison stared at the woman blankly. The words made no sense, yet she had a horrible creeping presentiment of disaster.

Miss Pringle studied her, avidly watching for her reaction. 'Oh yes, I can see you didn't know, and I hope the shock won't be too much, but I felt it was only my duty to let you know. Actually, they've been—very good friends indeed, shall we say—for the past few months. He would call in when you were away on your buying travels and take Miss Conrad out, and I used to say to myself, 'Now I wonder if that poor Miss Lennox knows what's going on?' But of course you didn't, did you?'

Alison's pallid face was answer enough. She felt with her hand for the dainty gilt chair behind her and sat down weakly. It was she herself who had purchased this chair, she thought, with numbed irrelevance. She had seen it in the window of an auction-room; a pretty little imitation French chair with carved legs and brocaded upholstery, just the thing for The Gilt Cabinet. She remembered how pleased Geralda had been. Now it struck her like a blow that, even at that time,

Geralda must have been pursuing her affair with Toby.

'You wouldn't like me to fetch you a glass of water?' Miss Pringle fussed. 'Poor dear, it has all been such a shock. But believe me, you're as well off without him. Anyway, I could never imagine what you saw in him—or Miss Conrad, for that matter. It really stuns me how she'd be bothered with someone like him—although, of course, he's very comfortably off.'

'Please go away,' Alison whispered. She wanted to be alone to try to create order out of the chaos that seemed to swirl in her head.

The woman from The Rose Bowl bridled angrily. 'Well, I must say you haven't much gratitude. It's not everyone who would have put themselves in the position I have and told the truth, unpleasant as it might be—'

'Oh do please, please go away,' Alison pleaded. 'Can't you see I want to think this over by myself?'

'Oh, very well, if that's how you feel!' And to Alison's relief she flounced from the shop.

Not for a moment did Alison doubt the truth of what she had been told. She had noticed a change in Toby's attitude towards her, but had not given it much thought. She had simply concluded that he was on the point of proposing and that the thought of the responsibilities he would have to face was making his manner rather withdrawn. But

13

now she could put a different interpretation on his changed demeanour. No doubt, she thought bitterly, he had been wondering how he could explain the fact that there was to be no engagement.

It also made sense of Geralda's somewhat ambiguous remarks before she had left the house. She felt a growing bitterness succeed the dull, numb ache of shock. So Geralda was trying to justify her treachery by suggesting that in the first place she had not loved Toby well enough for marriage. Well, even if that were true, it would not justify such a deception.

She sprang to her feet in agitation as she remembered that Toby would be arriving at any minute. She couldn't face him, she told herself desperately. Or would he come at all? Her mouth twisted in momentary bitterness. But of course he would! It was not in his nature to leave unfinished business where she was concerned. Was tonight, then, to be the night on which he was to break to her the news that everything was over between them? Strange how one's world could collapse within a few minutes! It was such a short time since she had set off, expecting an engagement ring, and had found herself with her life crashed in ruins about her.

Swiftly she slipped into her coat and pulled the door behind her, and when she had locked it, slipped the key into her bag and

14

hurried along the street. She felt a tremendous sense of relief that she had escaped a confrontation with Toby. She would go back to the flat. Geralda would have gone off by now with Mark. She would have the flat to herself: time to try to gather the shards together and begin afresh.

But when she did arrive back at the flat she found, to her dismay, that Geralda was still there. She lay sprawled in a chair, dressed in a black and silver trouser suit, her hair piled high.

'Imagine,' she exclaimed, so wrapped up in her own grievance that she showed no surprise at Alison's quick return, 'Mark phoned to say he can't manage it. No excuse, of course—but then that's Mark all over! I don't know why I put up with him. I'm getting sick of the bright young things. I think I'd settle for a staid middle-aged type any day.'

Alison drew off her coat. 'Someone like Toby Benson, perhaps?' she asked quietly.

She saw the look of shock as Geralda tilted her head towards her.

'So you've found out!'

'Yes, I've found out,' Alison replied quietly.

For a moment Geralda had the grace to look embarassed. 'I suppose it was that little sneak, Miss Pringle, who told you? I used to see her peering out from behind the petunias at us as we left the boutique.'

'There was no need to deceive me,' Alison said. 'You could have told me: it would have been kinder in the long run.'

'My dear good girl, how can one tell a girl that her boy-friend has fallen out of love with her? I mean, it's completely impossible and poor Toby's not the brave, romantic type. In fact, all in all, I think he's rather weak.'

'Then why did you bother taking him from me?' Alison asked in the cool, unemotional voice that seemed to disconcert Geralda more than a flaming scene.

'Because, my dear girl, I intend to marry him. That's why!'

'Marry him?'

'For heaven's sake, you don't think I'd go playing about with a drip like Toby Benson for amusement, do you? No, as I told you, I'm sick of the bright young men. I want to settle down. I've my head too well screwed on to think of marrying a playboy and leading a life of misery. No, Toby's kind and undemanding. He'll make an ideal husband. He'll do just what he's told. I don't intend to run The Gilt Cabinet until I'm an old, grey-haired lady—and anyway, I did get the strong impression that you didn't care for him particularly.'

'Poor Toby!' Alison laughed bitterly. 'He seems to be unfortunate in the girls he picks. But at least I thought I was in love with him.

You realised right from the beginning that you weren't.'

Geralda got to her feet and stalked back and forth across the room with smooth, cat-like steps. 'Don't take that line with me. When it comes to marriage a girl has to do the best for herself. If she allows herself to get too romantic she'll find she's married a no-good type. Very romantic and charming, of course, but without a brass farthing or the ability to make money. No, Toby is going places, and I intend gong with him.' She stopped in front of Alison and held out her hand. 'Look why don't you and I be friends? It's stupid to quarrel over someone like Toby. We've got on very well and the boutique is flourishing. You really are a genius when it comes to buying; you've got artistic flair, or something. Something that I haven't got anyhow! We'll make pots of money and, when it's made, we can quarrel then, but in the meantime, don't let Toby get between us.'

Alison shook her head. 'Oh no, this is the end, Geralda. I simply couldn't stay on knowing—knowing—' she couldn't add that she meant, knowing now that she couldn't believe a single word spoken by this girl whom she had believed to be her friend. 'No, I'm opting out.'

'You mean you're actually leaving me? Leaving the boutique just when it's doing remarkably well?' Geralda shrilled incredulously. 'But that's ridiculous. What will you do? Where will you go?'

'I'll go back to Abercorrey,' Alison said on sudden impulse, and immediately her spirits rose. Yes, she would go back again to Abercorrey, that strange household that she remembered from childhood.

'Abercorrey!' Geralda echoed. 'I used to hear you speak about it. It's terribly wild, isn't it; somewhere in the north of Scotland?'

'It's not really so wild,' Alison told her defensively.

'At least the village is not more than three miles away!' Geralda scoffed. 'My dear girl, do you realize what you're saying? How on earth do you think you'd stand it after the busy extrovert life you've been used to here? Why, you'd be bored stiff. You'd be screaming to get back before you're a week there—and anyway, if I remember, there's something peculiar about the set-up, wasn't there?'

'Mother and I didn't live at Abercorrey,' Alison evaded the question. 'We lived in a cottage in the grounds. Mrs Heseltine was a semi-invalid. She had been to school with Mother and when Daddy died she offered us the cottage. Mother was a sort of nurse-companion to her until—' She hesitated. Even yet she found it difficult to speak about that dreadful day when Ian Heseltine had drowned in the River Correy

18

and Mrs Heseltine had been discovered in her bedroom collapsed with a stroke from which she never was to recover. Most clearly of all she remembered Keith, his wild, ungovernable furies, the eyes that could sparkle with devilish laughter or darken like a storm-tossed loch; Keith, who was so unlike a Heseltine in every way, even to the shock of ebony hair that hung thick on his broad forehead. Keith, of course, had been blamed for his brother's death, for it was in keeping with his wild reckless temperament that he should have tempted the frail blond Ian to swim across the treacherous river. She remembered the bitter dislike with which Seaton Heseltine had afterwards regarded his son—but then Seaton, intellectual, reserved and indomitably proud, had never really understood this second son of his. The death of his heir had been a bitter blow; Ian, who had been so brilliant, the cleverest and most promising of all the Heseltines. But above all, as far as the father was concerned, had been the loss of the son who would have inherited Abercorrey, and Seaton had all the pride of race of a Highlander. She remembered how, afterwards, he had retreated into himself. Occasionally he would visit his stricken wife, stretched immobile in her vast bed, but it was with a sort of cold solicitude that was almost worse than neglect.

Then, with a little sense of shock, she

realized that Keith would now be a man and the heir to Abercorrey.

'Will you go back and live in the cottage?' Geralda asked. For the first time she regarded Alison with an air of genuine interest, for although she did not realize it, Alison's expression had been revealing.

'I suppose so,' she replied. 'It was understood, after Mother's death, that the cottage was to be at my disposal any time I needed it.'

'But you never went back, not even for a holiday!'

Alison hesitated. It was true, but then she had tried to shut out memories of Abercorrey. It had been a deliberate if perhaps not fully understood decision on her part. Almost defensively she said, 'Of course I could have gone back any time I wanted, but after I left Abercorrey I began an entirely new sort of life. Abercorrey seemed distant, like existence on another planet.'

'From what I've gathered the Heseltines seem to be a rather unusual family,' Geralda said. 'Not, of course, that you've ever confided in me. In fact, you've always been extremely reticent concerning your background.'

Perhaps the reason was that she had never really had a background, Alison thought a little wryly—at least, not a background in the accepted sense. Abercorrey had been the

20

tapestry into which their lives had been woven. For her mother and herself the great granite pile had been the centre of their existence and she remembered that even in the evenings, when her mother returned to the cottages set by the burn, how eagerly she would recount the day's events. Gradually, like a blurred picture coming into focus, Abercorrey came back to her with all its poignant memories. She could almost smell the scent of the heather and hear the bubbling lilt of the peat-stained burn.

'I suppose this Seaton Heseltine is a sort of laird or something?' Geralda asked, with typical vagueness.

'Well, yes, I suppose he is. He owns most of the land around the local village. They're a very old family and were on the side of the Stuarts during the rebellion. They have all sorts of mementoes of those days.'

'It sounds remarkably dismal,' Geralda said dryly.

Alison knew the remark was made derisively, but answered with perfect seriousness, 'Not dismal. The house is built of granite and is set against a background of mountains. In autumn the hills are ablaze with purple heather and golden gorse. At least that's the way I remember it, because that was the time of year when I left Abercorrey.'

Then gradually she found herself recalling

21

the past and subconsciously experienced a feeling almost of triumph as she realised that for once she was holding Geralda's engrossed attention as she recounted how, while her mother served as companion to the fretful Flora Heseltine, she, a schoolgirl, had hero-worshipped and tried to keep pace with Keith Heseltine, honoured if he would allow her to trudge after him as he stalked deer in the wild hills behind Abercorrey, or to sit quietly beside him as he fished in the Dee. Without being aware of it she had somehow conveyed the strange, wild spirit that had seemed at times to possess Keith Heseltine.

'He's probably settled down into a stodgy country gentleman by this time,' Geralda interposed. 'After all, there's a great deal of water under the bridge since you lived at Abercorrey.'

'Yes, it's seven years ago,' Alison said wonderingly. 'Hester must be nearly old enough to be married now, although it's hard to think of her except as a plump little kid with a solemn face, riding a Shetland pony.'

'And who's Hester?' Geralda asked a little impatiently. 'You seem to have been so wrapped up in Keith that you've forgotten the rest of the dramatis personae.'

Alison found herself blushing. It was ridiculous, of course, but she probably had been speaking more of Keith than she had intended to. But seven long years had passed for her too. She was no longer a hero-worshipping schoolgirl. Keith would be a man by now; perhaps married!

'Hester was the youngest of the Heseltines; she was a frightfully staid child and extraordinarily conventional in her outlook. She disapproved heartily of both Keith and myself, young as she was. She used to follow us around solemnly on a plump little Shetland pony, breathing disapproval. What I remember most distinctly about her is her extraordinary hair: it was very straight and the colour of sand.'

'Don't be too surprised if you find considerable changes at your romantic Scottish castle,' Geralda interposed. 'If you're really determined to go I'd write first if I were you and find out if the offer of the cottage still holds good before I tore off North.'

'Yes, I suppose I'd better,' Alison said flatly. Geralda's pessimistic pronouncement had brought her back to earth with a depressing thud. Strange how she had not visualized Abercorrey as changed in any way.

And she too was changed. She was no longer the worshipping schoolgirl at Keith's beck and call. She was a successful business-woman, capable of making well-judged decisions, highly successful in her own sphere of life. Or was she? She had failed dismally as far as Toby Benson was concerned. And then too, her blindness in not realizing she had lost him to Geralda. Well, at least Geralda had given her one piece of good advice! She wouldn't go tearing up to Scotland in the hope of being accepted on the old terms. She would prudently write and ascertain first of all if the offer of the cottage was still open.

Somehow she felt it would be. Seaton Heseltine was not given to impulsive gestures. He would have considered long and deliberately before offering her such a gift. But it was impossible to be sure.

But Geralda, as usual, had had the ability to raise doubts and conjectures, and Alison felt a sudden disenchantment with the whole scheme. Yet she knew that she must get away from the flat. It would be intolerable to have to face Toby's shamefaced apologies; to see Geralda and himself together would be unendurably humiliating.

No longer, however, had she any intention of rushing up North, and when she did write there was a long delay before she received a reply.

When at last the letter did arrive she felt a strange inexplicable sensation of trepidation as she slit open the envelope. The writing-paper was ostentatiously headed by the familiar Heseltine crest, a savage mask of a wildcat. She remembered how her mother had been secretly amused at Seaton's inordinate pride in his lineage. Her eyes scanned the writing that slanted across the thick white page, the words as stiff and unbending as the man himself. Of course his offer of the cottage still held good, he informed her, and there was the faint suggestion that by doubting his offer she had impugned his honour.

'I think you will find a good many changes if and when you arrive—some good, some unfortunate—but these you can discover for yourself when you reach Abercorrey.' Among the more propitious events he numbered his marriage to Morag Arnott. Her family, he informed Alison, with his usual emphasis on lineage, was distinguished and almost as old in tradition as the Heseltines themselves.

For a moment Alison wondered what type of woman had taken the place of her mother's friend, the gentle, self-effacing Flora Heseltine.

'I am particularly glad,' he pursued, 'you have decided to come back now, because Hester is of an age when I feel your influence would be beneficial. She has, I am afraid, changed a great deal in character and in her own quiet way is as big an outlaw as Keith—who, by the way, is now taking on the main burden of responsibility as far as Abercorrey is concerned.'

He ended by assuring her that she would get on well with the new Mrs Heseltine who was, he informed her, of sterling character.

When Alison laid down the letter she experienced a curious sensation of disappointment. It was foolish, she knew, to feel like this. What had she expected in a letter from Seaton Heseltine in the first place? she asked herself. Had she really hoped for a warm welcome from the austere Seaton Heseltine? But there had been something chilling in the information that she would be expected to act as a sort of duenna to his daughter, Hester, whom she remembered as a strange, silent child with pellucidly pale blue eyes. Even then she had had a strange inimical detachment that had been chilling in one so young. How would Hester react to her reappearance at Abercorrey? Alison wondered.

But fundamentally it was Keith who was foremost in Alison's mind: the gipsy-dark boy with the worn heath-stained kilt would be a man now. But time had not stood still for her either: when they met again she would view him with cool, unflinching detachment, she told herself.

Alison spent the following few days shopping for suitable clothes, for she intended to do a lot of walking during her visit to Abercorrey and she knew what the heather and bracken-covered moors could do to all but the stoutest clothing.

But occasionally during the intervening days she was annoyed to discover herself rehearsing exactly what reaction she would show when she met Keith Heseltine again. She must be careful to look upon her visit to Abercorrey as simply an interlude in her life—probably a fairly short one—in which she would renew old friendships without any particular emotion, and Keith must be firmly placed within those ranks, she told herself, as she packed a tweed skirt and thick ribbed sweater for she remembered how cold it could be at this time of the year at Abercorrey. Decisively she secured the lids of her suitcases—as decisively as she intended to dismiss Keith from her thoughts.

CHAPTER TWO

Heather was in bloom on the mountains as the train drew near to Aberdeen.

Before she had left for Scotland Alison had received a further letter from Seaton Heseltine in which he had informed her that his wife Morag would meet her at the station: old Hector Weir would be driving the car.

It was strange, Alison thought, how when she had been reviewing her memories of Abercorrey she had forgotten Hector, for surely Hector was not an easy person to overlook, with his beetle brows, faded red whiskers and the dusty tam-o'-shanter

27

without which it was impossible to visualise him. He was as much a part of Abercorrey as the dark fortress-like walls.

When at last the train drew to a halt Alison had no difficulty in recognising him. He appeared unchanged: even the tam-o'-shanter seemed to be of the original mould.

Beside him stood a very tall, gaunt woman in rough rust-coloured Harris tweeds and thickly ribbed stockings. She stared about, vague and anxious. Then as Hector pointed out Alison, Morag strode towards her, the thonged tongues on her shoes flapping wildly. She advanced a strong, bony-looking hand. 'I'm Morag Heseltine,' she announced. 'Seaton would have met you himself, but he's a little off-colour this weather and is taking it easy.'

She had a strange, awkward manner and now that she was close Alison could see that her cheeks were weather-beaten as though Morag spent a great deal of her time striding over the moors in all sorts of weathers. It was clear that the new Mrs Heseltine was not given to practising the social graces and for a moment Alison wondered fleetingly how the snobbish Seaton Heseltine was reacting to this trait in his wife's character.

The she became aware of Hector's small blinking eyes fixed on her with something as near amiability as he was capable of. 'You're welcome back, Miss Alison,' he announced.

28

'Although you'll find a few changes at the old hame that you didn't expect.'

'Yes, I suppose there have been a few changes,' Morag said vaguely as she led the way back to the car.

'Aye, yon Tibbie Lochart, for one thing,' he announced grimly as he got behind the wheel. 'I can't think what the Master was thinking of, asking her to settle down in Abercorrey. Nothing but trouble she causes: always speering and clyping on a body.'

Alison was aware that Morag was gazing at her a little nervously as she said hurriedly, 'You take poor Tibbie much too seriously, Hector. After all, she does keep to her own part of the house—more or less.'

Tibbie Lochart! Alison tried to pin down her memories of that dim figure from the past. A distant relation of Seaton's, Tibbie was a faded little lady with bright blue eyes who used occasionally to visit Abercorrey. Ian had been her favourite and always before she departed she used to present him with one of her weird paintings on velvet. The subject was invariably the same—a rose—but in such strange colours that they used to reduce Ian to tears of laughter—blue roses, splashed with mauve and cerise, or orange roses with carmine and black: such roses as never were on land or sea. Along with the rose painting she used to slip him a pound from her meagre income, for as far as Tibbie was concerned,

29

Ian, the eldest of the Heseltines and quite grown up, was still only a child. He used to pocket the pound with imperturbable aplomb, giving Tibbie in reward the slight sweet smile that charmed all who came in contact with him.

'Drive up Union Street, Hector, and we'll pick up Hester,' Morag was saying.

It had been raining and now as they drove past the grey stone shops shafts of sun made the quartz in the granite shine like diamonds.

'I'm sorry Hester wasn't with us when we met you,' Morag continued with that same faintly apologetic air that seemed to stamp her, 'but you know what young girls are! She insisted on taking the opportunity to do some shopping.'

By way of something to say, Alison remarked, 'Hester must be quite grown up now.'

'Yes, almost sixteen. It will be splendid for her to have someone like you staying at Abercorrey. There is so little company of her own age in this part of the country and she can be—well, rather difficult at times. It's natural, I suppose, that she should resent me, but it does make my position extremely difficult—more difficult than Seaton realizes, but then he's rather a bookworm and now that Keith has taken over the management of the estate he spends most of his time in the library—that is when he's well enough to

30

come downstairs. He's such a reserved sort of person.' She sighed with an air of resignation. 'But of course I needn't tell you. After all, so much of your childhood was spent at Abercorrey. I expect there's very little you don't know of the family.'

She stopped speaking and frowned ahead, but Alison got the impression that what Morag had said had been stored up for a long time and that her silence was not due to the realization that she had been indiscreet in her revelations to someone who was more or less a complete stranger to her but rather that she was milling over an ever-present problem, one to which so far she had found no solution.

Hector stopped the car outside what Alison remembered to be one of Aberdeen's most exclusive shops: in the windows single articles of women's clothing were draped elegantly against pillars or laid reverently on a rich dark velvet background.

They waited for quite a while, making small-talk, and, as time passed and there was no sign of Hester, Morag asked Hector if he would go in and fetch her.

'Indeed, I willnae,' Hector growled. 'I wouldnae go into they shops full of female gewgaws and the like rubbish if you paid me a million pounds.'

It was at this point that Hester emerged bearing a large striped blue and white dress-box. There was no possibility of mistaking her: she was taller now and the thick sturdiness of youth had been replaced by a slim willowy figure, but the white expressionless face was as secretive as ever and the sand-coloured hair was smoothly combed back from her wide forehead and hung in a shimmering curtain about her shoulders. There was a strange distinction about her closed, reserved face that was immediately noticeable.

When she reached the car she showed little interest in Alison's presence. She nodded briefly. 'So you've come back,' she said. 'I didn't think you would.'

Alison found this salutation disconcerting to say the least of it and, embarrassed, she found herself asking brightly, 'But why should you think that? I've always loved Abercorrey.'

Hester laughed shortly as she settled herself into the car. 'You mean you loved Keith.'

Alison found herself flushing crimson at the unexpectedness of the attack. 'I don't know what you mean.'

'Don't you? Then why were you always tagging after him when you lived here? You were like his shadow. We all knew you were crazy about him.'

Alison was conscious of Hector's large ears almost twitching with interest and disapproval as he eased the car into the busy street, but Hester seemed either unconscious of, or indifferent to, his outrage, or her step-mother's almost tangible confusion at such outspokenness.

'I suppose you thought no one guessed, but we all knew you were crazy about him. Ian and I used to laugh when we'd see you plodding after him. Ian used to say—' She stopped with a short choking sound and Alison remembered how bitterly she had resented her elder brother's death. Her vitriolic attack had betrayed Hester into an intolerable memory. It was she too who had witnessed Ian's death and had rushed back to the house with the horrifying news.

'Did you buy anything interesting, dear?' Morag intervened with an air of spurious interest.

It was so clear that it was an attempt to change the conversation that Hester made no effort to hide her contempt for the obvious strategy.

'Since when have you become interested in clothes?' she inquired, fixing her eyes meaningly on the rust-coloured Harris tweed.

'Morag laughed uneasily. 'Oh, I know I'm no judge of pretty things, but I do like the clothes you wear, although somehow I always feel more at home in tweeds.'

'Obviously,' Hester replied briefly, and relapsed into a brooding silence.

The country was wild and heather-covered and from a distance Alison could see the huge pile of Abercorrey etched against the sky: as they drew near a shaft of light splintered through the clouds and glittered on the granite blocks that formed the massive outer walls. It was just as she remembered it and Alison found herself tremble with emotion as they drew nearer. It was as though not a day had passed since she had left Abercorrey. An incline of closely clipped grass sloped sharply down from the foundations, the rich greenness a striking contrast to the dour, uncompromising grey of the building.

The corbie-stepped roofs of the gables were like giant square teeth and here and there, as though they had been formed without any particular plan or purpose, elaborate oriel windows hung from the walls suported by ornate corbels depicting the Heseltine crest; carved roughly in the granite the very primitiveness of the workmanship made the ferocious cat-mask almost evil in its malignity.

They drove past the front of the house and underneath an arch into a wide courtyard.

As she got out of the car Alison gazed up almost instinctively at the windows of the rooms above the archway. It was here Flora had passed the last few months of her life as she could no longer bear to remain in the rooms that faced over the river that had claimed her favourite son.

As they entered the great hall Alison was

overcome by a flood of memories: even to the least article of furniture it seemed to be exactly as she remembered it. The great bronze sconces still stood on either side of the vast chimneypiece and against the rough stone walls were displayed the tattered remnants of decayed tartans and banners borne by long-dead Heseltines on Scotland's fields of battle. Here were precious links with Bannockburn, Flodden, Prestonpans and finally Culloden in which the Heseltines had remained staunchly Stuart in their sympathies. How often had she seen Keith Heseltine thoughtfully pass from one relic to another, brooding on past glories.

He had delighted too in explaining the contents of the glass case which stood in one of the corners: a strand of blond hair that had been Bonnie Prince Charlie's: a signet ring that had belonged to Mary Stuart: odds and ends of history that had, at the time, been to Alison no more than musty and rather pathetic mementoes.

But it was the furniture that was most evocative. As a girl Alison had been fascinated by the massive dark Jacobean tables and chests with their heavy carved griffins bearing in their mouths large brass rings.

It was into this hall too that Hester had rushed, her face blank with shock, to tell of Ian's drowning.

35

'You're welcome back to Abercorrey, Miss Alison,' Jennie McVey interrupted her rather depressing train of thought.

And she too was part of the past, Alison thought, for when Alison had been last at Abercorrey Jennie had been a housemaid. Now she stood upright and self-possessed, dressed in the severe black that denoted her position as housekeeper.

'I'm glad to be back, Jennie,' Alison replied.

'I'd have known you right away,' Jennie continued. 'You havenae changed that much.'

'Nor you, Jennie,' Alison replied.

But there was a subtle change in Jennie, apart from her new status, for the small sly eyes were even more cunning than Alison had remembered them, and she had still too an almost perpetual smirk.

'And now perhaps I'd better show you to your room,' Jennie said briskly. 'Hector will bring in your things.'

As she spoke Hector came into the hall with Alison's suitcases in his arms. 'Her things are already brung in,' he said grimly to Jennie. 'There'll be no need for you to give orders.'

Hector's tone and the scowl that accompanied his words showed that he disliked Jennie intensely.

It was also clear from the satisfied smirk that crossed Jennie's face as she turned away

36

that the housekeeper took delight in upsetting him: his detestation pleased and satisfied her instead of annoying her.

It was with a feeling of relief that Alison accompanied Jennie upstairs. She had assumed that she would be staying at the cottage in the grounds which she had shared with her mother and now she realized that subconsciously she had been dreading the isolation and the poignant memories that could not but crowd upon her alone in that spot. It would be wonderful to be enclosed in the big house for the night, feeling the companionship of other people under the same roof. It would be for the night only, she supposed. On the following day, Seaton, his strict code of hospitality satisfied, would probably arrange for her to move to the cottage.

So engrossed was she in these thoughts that she did not notice where Jennie's footsteps were leading. It was only when the housekeeper stopped before a familiar door, the panels carved in intricate patterns in which the familiar wild-cat symbol of the Heseltines was incorporated, that Alison drew back with a little gasp. 'But this is Flora—Mrs Heseltine's—room,' she protested.

'And what of it?' Jennie asked, regarding her with a steady, curiously knowledgeable gaze as she put her hand to the amber handle and turning it ushered Alison into the room.

Alison stood just inside the doorway surveying the familiar room: the half-tester bed; the antique walnut furniture, the beading ornamented with a tiny design of gold and inlaid with a narrow line of black wood; the long windows, rather narrow for the size of the room. It was from one of those narrow windows overlooking the swift-flowing Correy that Flora must have witnessed the drowning of her beloved elder son. This was the room in which she had fallen down in the stroke from which she was never really to recover in spite of Mrs Lennox's devoted nursing.

'Not this room, Jennie,' Alison said, a note of urgency in her voice. 'What would Mr Heseltine say if he thought that I—'

'Oh, dinna fash yourself,' Jennie said with a sort of airy familiarity. 'The master himself gave orders that you were to be put here.'

Alison gazed at her for a moment in stunned amazement, but Jennie, as though unaware of her regard, moved across the room and busied herself straightening the old-fashioned duchess set that, slightly yellowed by age, but newly laundered, lay upon the dressing-table. 'My, they girls nowadays, you cannae get them to do anything right,' Jennie said with a great show of pre-occupation as she smoothed the strip of lace and re-arranged the tortoiseshell-backed brushes and comb that had once been Flora Heseltine's.

'I'll go in and see Mr Seaton as soon as I've tidied myself,' Alison broke the lengthening silence.

She was astonished as Jennie swung around from the dressing-table, saying briskly, 'I'll no have you seeing him the noo, Miss Alison. He's not up to it. Later on perhaps, if he's feeling better in the evening.'

Alison's first impulse was to protest, but there was something so authoritative in Jennie's manner that she bit back her retort and said stiffly, 'Whenever he feels ready to see me, then.'

She was conscious that her manner showed the resentment she felt, and was aware too that Jennie as she crossed to the door regarded this first encounter as a triumph for herself. It was important to her that Alison, the daughter of the woman who had once held a position of some authority in the house, should recognise her new status. By forbidding Alison to see Seaton without her permission she had achieved her point.

Shortly afterwards Alison's cases were brought up by a bright-faced young boy, the son of one of the gardeners, he informed Alison as he briskly pocketed the tip she gave him.

Alison unpacked in a leisurely way. There was nothing to hurry about any longer.

39

Instead, she was exercised in her mind as to how she would pass the time until dinner. She woud walk into the village and see what changes had occurred in Correybrae, she decided. She changed into a tweed skirt and put on one of the jumpers she had purchased with the Highlands in mind. Both were in shades of soft blue and greens that toned and gave a curiously misty effect that was becoming.

From a drawer in the dressing-table she took out the small enamelled silver box in which she kept her hoard of jewellery. There were a few antique pieces which she had picked up cheap; cameo brooches and a couple of the jewelled insects which seemed to fascinate the Victorians and which went so well with modern clothes; a long double necklace of jet. There were modern pieces too; a giant glittering zircon, the cold rays unnaturally bright; a small strand of pearls which she usually wore with her more conservative clothes.

She decided to wear one of her favourite brooches; a double bar of gold from which hung a single drop pearl.

As she was replacing the box she accidentally knocked it against the edge of the drawer: it slipped from her fingers and the contents were strewn on the worn and faded dark green carpet. She knelt to retrieve the articles and found herself groping for one of the chunks of cairngorm that had rolled away. As she held it in her hand, noting how the soft yellow streaks merged into the grey-brown of the opaque quartz, she wondered why she had kept these lumps of stone through the years she had been away.

Vividly she remembered Keith giving them to her. He had come along to the cottage one evening, had thrown pebbles up at her window and when she had run downstairs and slipped out by the back entrance she had found him waiting for her in the shadow of the giant clipped holly hedge that enclosed the tiny garden of the cottage, separating it from the grounds of Abercorrey.

'Where have you been?' she had greeted him in a whisper, for there had been great excitement at Abercorrey over the fact that he had disappeared without trace for several days.

'Never you mind,' he had replied in the rough vernacular speech that he affected, chiefly because it annoyed Ian and Hester.

'They've been searching for you everywhere,' she had told him.

'Let them,' he had replied briefly. 'Here, I got these for you.'

'Oh!' Her exclamation had been one of disappointment, as he had thrust the rough, unpleasing stones into her hands.

'They're cairngorms,' he had told her. 'Jewels, though they don't look like it now.

41

Some day I'll have them polished and made into a bracelet for you.'

'So that's where you've been, climbing in the mountains!' she had gasped. 'Wait till your father hears—'

'You're not to clype on me or I'll never forgive you,' he had hissed in her ear. 'Promise, or I'll take my bracelet back.'

'You can keep your old bracelet,' she had scoffed.

Nevertheless she had kept the stones.

And of course she had not told on him: admidst all the speculation, the scoldings and uproar that had greeted his return she had been silent, hugging to herself the knowledge that she alone held the secret of those days when he had been climbing in the vast, trackless wastes of the Cairngorms.

Ever since she had kept those rough chunks of stone. Why? Why? she wondered. And as she put them slowly back into her jewellery box she knew that soon she would know the answer: soon she would meet once again the boy who had given her that childish gift and she would know—Know what? she asked herself a little sternly. Know whether that first love of youth had in fact been the one great love of her life, or a foolish girlish infatuation which she would put behind her when, this time, she left Abercorrey for ever.

Slowly Alison closed the door of Flora's room behind her and made her way along the shadowed corridors. How deeply they contrasted with the brightly lit and gleaming places in which Toby had entertained her before Geralda had come between them! There had been dinners in the softly-lit, deeply-carpeted dining rooms of exclusive hotels and restaurants: there had been evenings at the ballet or a new play with supper afterwards, the sound of canned music a background to the trite, rather ponderous conversation that Toby considered suitable for an evening out.

Now as she entered a dim passage, the wood panelling filmed with dust and only faintly reflecting the dim light from a window at the end, she had a curious feeling of homecoming. This was the place she belonged to, she was thinking. The years she had spent in England had only been an interlude. And she breathed a silent, almost unconscious prayer that somehow or other she might be allowed to stay.

She nearly gave a scream as a tiny figure appeared before her. For a moment Alison thought the pale form was that of a child, then a faint shaft of light fell upon the worn, lined face and Alison knew that this was Tibbie Lochart.

Had Tibbie always been as small as this? was Alison's first startled reaction. Tibbie had a tiny head in keeping with her diminutive figure and to her mouth she held a forefinger

43

no larger than a child's in a gesture of conspiracy. But the round ingenuous childlike eyes which peered into Alison's face were exactly as she remembered them.

'You've changed a great deal: quite a grown-up young lady, now,' Tibbie greeted Alison. 'But I knew you right away. I was waiting for you, you know, because I wanted to find out if you are trustworthy.'

The little woman had drawn very close and her manner was so strange that Alison found herself drawing back involuntarily.

'Oh, you needn't be afraid of *me*,' Tibbie assured her. 'But there is one here whom you'd be well advised to steer clear of. Take my warning: be on your guard.'

'What—what do you mean?' Alison stammered.

'Beware of an evil woman,' Tibbie said so dramatically that it struck Alison that the little woman was enjoying the effect she was creating.

'Yes, yes, I'll do that,' Alison said with an attempt at brisk common sense, moving forward as she spoke.

'You don't believe me, I see,' Tibbie said shrewdly as Alison attempted to edge past her. 'But you'll think differently when you've seen my paintings. I brought them all with me to Abercorrey, you know, and I've done lots more since I came. You must come up to my studio in the attics and I'll show you

44

paintings no one else has ever seen. That's because I know I can trust you. I had to make sure of that first. Oh yes, you'll be very interested. I hardly ever do roses now, you know. Oh no, nowadays I do much more interesting subjects.'

'I'd like to see them some time,' Alison told her, 'but at the moment I'm going for a walk.'

'Then you won't come now!' Tibbie said wistfully. Then, more cheerfully, she went on, 'However, I can wait. Some day you'll come to look at them—you'll feel you must.' And with a curious little bob of her tiny head she scuttled away and seemed to melt into the shadows of the corridors.

Alison was glad to leave the confines of the great house and to take the broad path by the river where already leaves had drifted down from the trees and lay wet and dark brown in the mud.

Soon the little hamlet of Correybrae came into view, the small houses built of stone with high flat fronts, smallish windows and narrow gables, set in terraces of three or four. As she drew near the little kirk, built of granite too like everything else in the hamlet, she heard organ music and drawn by the sound slipped through the door which stood ajar and sat in one of the pews listening appreciatively. From the back of the church she could not see the organist, but she did not need to look to discover who it was. She recognised that magic touch on the keys. The player, she knew, was Lowrie Inglis, once the village dominie, long since retired. The music he was playing was from Handel's 'Messiah', and as she listened scenes of her childhood flooded back to her. Vividly she remembered how, during one of the services she had sat electrified, half appalled, half admiring, while Keith carved his initials in one of the pews. They would still be there. Later, when the music ceased she would look at them.

It was at this point in her thoughts that something cold and rough was pressed into the back of her neck and she rose to her feet with a startled scream to find herself gazing into the bright blue eyes of a little boy who was holding a toy gun in his hand.

The music stopped with a discordant crash of notes and Lowrie Inglis hurried towards them.

'I've caught a spy, Great-uncle,' piped the child. 'I saw her sneaking in when she thought no one was looking and hiding in the back pew, but I've got her covered with my machine-gun and she can't escape!' He had a broad bulging forehead, curling carroty hair, and was liberally beplastered with freckles.

'Dear me, what are you up to now, Simon?' protested the old man. 'I can't take my eyes off you for as much as a minute but you get up to some mischief. I apologise, my dear,' he said to Alison. 'But he has been seeing too many of those blood-and-thunder stories—or whatever takes their place on TV nowadays. The children think of nothing but war and violence, and no one can keep this particular child in order but his father, and he has gone into Aberdeen today.' Then as his eyes studied her more closely, 'Why you're Alison Lennox! We heard you were to come to Abercorrey on holiday. Welcome home.'

As she shook hands with the old dominie Alison was thinking sadly that he had aged greatly since she had left Correybrae.

'I always knew you'd come back to us, Alison Lennox,' the old man said, smiling, as they left the kirk together. 'And what do you think of us now that you have returned? Seaton is sadly changed, of course, but at last he is permitting Keith to take on his natural responsibilities, and that is a good thing. Keith is decisive and energetic and I feel sure he will make a fine job of the management of Abercorrey. Seaton wouldn't listen to me when I urged him to take this step years ago, for I always liked the boy: there was never anything mean or underhand about him. All his faults were on the surface. But 'give a dog a bad name and hang him' as the saying goes. Still, it's only natural that Seaton should have been shattered by the tragedy. Even to this day he can't get over it. But of course it would have been the first thing you would notice as soon as you saw him again.'

'I haven't met Seaton yet,' Alison said a little defensively as he waited for her reply. 'He was too tired to see me when I arrived.'

'Ah yes, Jennie advised him to rest, no doubt,' the old man said dryly. 'Well, I wish my nephew was here to meet you now,' he hurried on, as though feeling he had made a faux pas. 'His wife died some time ago, leaving this poor child motherless.' He nodded towards his great-nephew who had run on before them and was sweeping the bushes with his gun as he passed in make-believe of shooting down flocks of birds. 'I'm afraid my nephew spoils the lad—still it's only understandable in the circumstances. I persuaded him to bring Simon here with him for a holiday and I hope to keep him with me until he feels better and is able to take up the threads of his life again. Not, I must say, that David parades his grief or makes himself a weight on the company. No, the fault with him is that he keeps it to himself, and of course an old man like myself is no use to a broken-hearted man. It's a sympathetic ear from a woman he needs at the moment.'

As he spoke he eyed Alison, and she was under no illusions about the part he hoped she would play in his nephew's restoration to cheerful spirits.

She shook hands with the old dominie before they parted and Simon came

48

gambolling up to demand a handshake too. Laughingly Alison bent down to take the grubby paw he proffered.

'I'm glad you've come back to Correybrae,' Simon announced. 'You're much nicer than Hester, and prettier too. She hates little boys. She's always scolding me and I don't like her. I hope Daddy marries you instead.'

'Simon, how can you be so bold!' the old man gasped. 'Now apologise nicely and run away before you say something else you oughtn't to.'

'I don't know that he should be made to apologise,' Alison laughed. 'At least, not for saying I'm pretty.'

'No, I suppose Simon should not be punished for speaking the truth,' Lowrie agreed with a twinkle. 'You were a pretty girl when you left here and you've come back even prettier—and an attractive and charming young woman as well.'

This was the sort of old-world compliment the dominie was accustomed to pay women, Alison knew, yet as she turned towards Abercorrey there was a new spring in her step and a brighter colour in her cheeks.

How badly she had needed that reassurance, she thought with a little wry twist to her lips. Since Toby had let her down so badly she had felt a humiliating loss of self-esteem.

That little glow of renewed confidence was

still with her as she entered the hall and on an impulse she crossed to the great wall mirror with its ebony frame and stood before it studying herself critically. Her small-boned face with its irregular features was slightly touched with pink after her walk in the clear air, her dark hair, always her best feature, was elegantly styled and curved over her brow in high waves and curls. Scottish hair, she thought, a little smile touching her lips, dark and misty, curling and vibrant. Celtic hair, one might call it—

'No need to look so pleased with yourself,' a deep, yet somehow familiar voice said at her shoulder. 'You're no beauty; nothing to set the Correy on fire. Just pretty, nothing more.'

Keith's eyes were regarding her in the mirror; his dark face looked over her shoulder with brooding attention.

She swung around to face him, flushed with anger and humiliation. 'I'm well aware I'm no beauty—never was and never will be. At least I've sense enough to know that.' She drew a deep breath and launched her attack. 'But at least I haven't gone off as much as *you* have!'

The instant the words were spoken she bit her lip in annoyance. It was such a silly, childish sort of jeer. It was true that he had grown into a strongly built, broad-shouldered man, dark-complexioned but marked with the scar on the side of his forehead which

50

remained from the great gash he had received on the day Ian was drowned. The boyish brightness had faded from his cheeks, leaving him with a brown weathered complexion that spoke of much time spent in the open air.

But these things were only what she would have expected. What then made him seem like a stranger to her? And then she decided it was the expression in his eyes. The sparkle, that touch of devilishness that had betokened boyish mischief, had disappeared; in their place was a sombre, brooding, almost melancholy expression. This was a man who seldom smiled, and never laughed, she knew instantly; a man upon whom the icy ostracism he had suffered after the death of his elder brother had left its mark.

His eyes bored into hers as he said, 'Whatever the improvement in your appearance—and it's certainly very slight—there has been no improvement whatsoever in your character. You're still the same bad-tempered spitfire, all claws and prickles, so don't try to pretend you've turned into a young lady, for you don't deceive me in the least.'

CHAPTER THREE

'Although I'm partial to spitfires, I insist on beauty in my future bride, I'm afraid. Mere prettiness, however attractive, won't do.'

Alison gave a gasp of indignation. He was deliberately provoking her, she was aware, but somehow or other she seemed to slip instantly into the contending attitude that had been hers during their youth. 'Why, I wouldn't marry you if you were the last man alive!' she found herself blurting, much to her discomfiture as she realized how childish and naïve the remark seemed.

'In which case I take it that you haven't come back with the intention of discovering how time had treated me. You weren't anxious to discover if I had turned into a tall, well-formed, blond man with well chiselled features and a charming, rather whimsical manner?' He sounded sardonic.

She was silent, looking at him in dismay. This was a description of Ian. How could she tell him that she had never been interested in Ian, who seem to have charmed everyone else?

'Instead, you find me grown coarse, blocky, unattractive, uncouth, scarred, and a murderer to boot.'

For a long moment Alison looked at him in silence. In his dark, brooding eyes, she read the misery he was too proud to show, and for an instant her whole mood softened towards him. But she knew that the smallest show of pity would be fatal. Instead she said coldly,

'You may be sure my coming back had nothing to do with you. I'm not the smallest bit interested in you or anything to do with you.'

'Then why have you come back?' he asked. 'What would make a pretty, sophisticated girl—even if she does lack true beauty—leave the attractions of England to make her way to this desolate, uninhabited, isolated, melancholy spot? Why does a girl suddenly seek the wide open spaces in preference to the gaiety and bustle of London? There is only one possible answer—an unsatisfactory love affair! You were deeply in love, were perhaps on the point of getting married, when you discovered that your intended had feet of clay. Is that the answer?'

Alison drew in her breath in a little gasp of dismay. Amongst other changes in Keith Heseltine appeared to be a new perspicacity, an awareness of other people and their problems that had not been in the boy she had left.

'So I'm right. You *have* had an unhappy love affair and you've come back here to Abercorrey to forget.'

'Nonsense,' Alison attempted a feeble defensive action.

But he ignored her. 'Now the best way for a girl to forget is to find someone on the rebound, and I'm exercising my mind about whom in the district you might find

53

interesting. There's only one man in the district for you—David Inglis, old Lowrie Inglis's nephew. And I must warn you that here you'll come up against competition in the person of Hester. She sees it as only a short while until the widower leads her to the altar.'

'But Hester's only sixteen,' Alison found herself exclaiming. 'Surely there must be a great difference in their ages.'

'We Heseltines are precocious in many ways,' he informed her. 'Young as she is, she is pursuing him with all the dark relentless passion of the Heseltines—to his annoyance, amusement, irritation and desperation. Hester scorns subtlety in the chase. The old-fashioned idea than the man prefers to be the hunter she regards with all the scorn of the modern girl. My own idea is that she is alienating him more and more, so perhaps there may be a chance for you there after all. If you play your cards cleverly, being careful to be docile and bending in contrast to Hester's aggressiveness, it's just possible you may be able to catch him.'

Alison moved towards the staircase. 'I've told you that I'm not interested in anyone here in Abercorrey—'

'Least of all are you interested in me,' he added mockingly.

'As I've already told you,' she snapped as she began to climb the stairs.

'Oh, yes, you wouldn't marry me if I were the last man alive on earth,' he repeated her remark.

'Exactly,' she turned to glare down defiantly at him as he stood at the foot of the stairs, his dark face upturned to her, the scar showing clearly in the shaft of light from one of the long windows.

She turned from the enigmatic, unsmiling gaze of those unfathomable eyes and ran lightly upstairs.

She had changed and was about to go downstairs again when there was a light perfunctory knock on her door and Jennie appeared.

'Mr Seaton will see you for a few minutes before dinner,' she informed Alison with the manner of one conferring a favour. 'He was going to go down to dinner in honour of your coming, but I wouldn't permit it. He's not really up to it. He doesn't realize how weak he is.'

In silence Alison followed her along the corridors towards Seaton's room which was in another wing of the great house. Here she found Seaton seated in a winged armchair near a blazing fire, a rug around his knees although the evening was mild. She was appalled by how frail and aged he had become since she had last seen him. The change in his appearance only served to emphasise the fact that Ian had so closely resembled his father.

It was from Seaton that Ian had inherited his slender patrician build, his fair good looks, fine features, pale skin and pale blue eyes.

'Now you're not to tire yourself out talking to Miss Alison,' Jennie told him severely, as she adjusted the cushions behind him.

'Thank you, Jennie,' Seaton replied, 'you're very kind.' He did not seem to resent her officious manner, Alison noticed with surprise. Seaton, as she remembered him, would have been the first to reject such fussiness and her assumption of being in command.

When at last Jennie flaunted from the room with a warning glance at Alison, signifying that she was not to tire Seaton by remaining too long, he gave Alison a hint of his new attitude towards the girl who was now in the position of housekeeper at Abercorrey.

'Jennie is a wonderful girl,' he said in his thin precise tones. 'She has taken on the full responsibilities of the house and makes light of the difficulties. But we value her more perhaps because she is a link with the past. She was a young girl here when my wife was alive and she's utterly devoted to the family.' He seemed pleased at her rather bossy ways and seemed to take them as an expression of her devotion.

'I'm sure she will make you comfortable,' he went on in his formal manner. 'If there is anything you lack let her know and I'm sure she will put herself out to make your stay with us as pleasant as possible.'

Did this mean that she would be expected to stay on at Abercorry during her visit? Alison wondered. 'I'm very comfortable,' she told him, then added, 'I've been given the room which was formerly Mrs Heseltine's.' Her expression showed her surprise at being given that room which she had always thought would never be used again.

There was a silence for a long moment while Seaton fixed her with his curious light blue eyes, eyes that seemed to be looking past her to some prospect that he alone could see. 'Yes, that was my idea,' he said at last. 'I thought it would be a fitting place for you during your stay.'

This statement surprised Alison even more. What on earth did he mean? But when he did not elaborate she said cautiously, 'Do you mean me to stay on here at Abercorrey, then? Or am I to move to the cottage in a few days?'

'The cottage is yours, of course,' he replied instantly. 'It was your mother's and yours for as long as ever you require it, but I'm sorry to say that during your absence it has fallen somewhat into disrepair. It would take a little while to put it in suitable order for you to live there again. But, if that is what you wish, I shall have the work put in hand immediately. However, I had hoped that you would be satisfied to stay here at the house, where you are very welcome indeed.'

He was silent for a long space after this and Alison, fearing she was overtiring him, was about to make her excuses and leave when he looked up abruptly from the fire upon which his gaze had been fixed. 'Have you met Keith since your return?' he asked abruptly.

'Yes,' Alison replied. The short angry monosyllable spoke volumes and Seaton sighed. 'So he has been rude to you already, has he?'

'Yes, very rude,' she replied, flushing angrily at the memory of some of Keith's more searching thrusts.

'And you resent it?' he asked softly.

Her flashing angry glance was sufficient answer.

Again there was a pause and this time Alison waited in silence. She had a curious feeling that Seaton, to whom words came so easily, was for once picking his way carefully about what he would say next. At length he said softly, 'I'm sorry you seem to be disagreeing already. You see, I had a hope—a hope that you might be the one person in the world with whom my son would get along. It seems you understood each other when you were hardly more than children and when I knew that you were coming back I hoped that you, as a grown woman, might be able to make allowances for him when no one else can—not even I myself, who am his father.'

Alison waited, her breath curiously restricted. What was Seaton about to say? she wondered. Instinctively she knew it was something that would be of great importance to her.

'"Give a dog a bad name and hang him." That is the saying, isn't it? So Lowrie Inglis tells me. I'm tired of being told of my injustice to this younger son of mine. But who can blame me?' he cried out suddenly in a loud voice. Then immediately lowering his tone, 'How would Lowrie feel, I wonder, about a son who had robbed him of everything he held dear in life? But I took his words to heart. I am giving Keith a chance to rehabilitate himself. I have given the total management of Abercorrey into his hands and we'll see how he'll comport himself now that he has responsibilities.'

Alison looked at him curiously. Seaton might have taken Lowrie Inglis's strictures to heart, she was thinking, but never would he forgive this son who had robbed him of his favourite son and of his wife almost in one hour.

'Keith is wild and unmanageable now that he is a man, just as he was as a boy,' Seaton said in a low, bitter voice. 'His behaviour is not what one would expect from a Heseltine. No company is too low for him to cultivate, and that is why I hoped—' he regarded her again steadily for a moment, and now she

59

understood only too clearly why she had been given that room which had once been his wife's. Why she was being urged to stay on at the house instead of moving into the cottage which everyone at Abercorrey regarded as her own property. Seaton hoped that she alone of all women would be able to understand this strange, unmanageable son of his, that the love she had once had for him would endure into womanhood and that she might come to regard Keith as her future husband.

Looking upon Seaton, now so shrunk and feeble in appearance, she felt a moment's pity. How she wished to reassure him—to be able to tell him that she still felt for the grown-up Keith what she had felt as a girl, but this could not be, and it would be dishonest to pretend that it could.

'It's true that there was a sort of friendship between us when we were young,' she replied slowly. 'But Keith has changed, you know. He's not the boy I knew then—nor am I the girl who left here all those years ago. We've both suffered a lot in the meanwhile and we've grown apart. I feel I no longer understand Keith and I'm sure he feels the same about me.'

She did not put into words the thought that slipped through her mind for a moment and then was lost—the thought that Seaton himself had helped to kill the merry-eyed, adventurous, generous-hearted boy that

60

Keith had been, and that his father's mistrust and hatred had helped to bring into being the morose, anti-social being who was now Keith Heseltine.

Seaton sighed. 'Well, it was only an idea,' he said.

'If you feel you no longer care for him there's nothing more to be said. If you'd prefer to stay at the cottage during your stay we can get it put in order for you, of course, but I don't think you should let this conversation between us make any difference to you. Everything I have said to you is in the strictest confidence, and I'm sure I have no need to urge you not to repeat anything that has passed between us. Now I won't keep you any longer. It must be almost dinner time. You'll excuse me if I don't join you this evening, but I think Jennie's right and I am more tired than I realize.'

As Alison went softly towards the door his eyes were closed, an expression of fatigue making his features even more drawn than usual.

As she drew the door open she let out a startled exclamation, for Jennie was just rising to her feet. It was only too clear that she had been kneeling outside the door eavesdropping on their conversation.

'Jennie!' she cried. How much of that very confidential conversation had Jennie overheard? She glanced back into the big room. Seaton seemed to be dozing at the fire which was at the other side of the room. They had spoken softly most of the time. Surely Jennie could not have heard very much to compensate her for her uncomfortable vigil outside the door.

Jennie smoothed her skirt with a gesture that was a little flurried. 'I was just about to come in and warn you you were staying too long,' she said, meeting Alison's eye defiantly. 'The Master mustn't be overtired, and I'll thank you to remember that—honoured guest though you may be.'

'And where's Seaton? Is he not coming down to dinner?' Morag asked as they gathered in the hall for a pre-dinner drink.

'Naw, he doesnae feel up to it this evening,' Hector answered as he handed around drinks.

'You mean, Jennie felt he wasn't up to it,' Morag replied bitterly as she reached a glass from the silver tray.

Only Morag, Keith and Alison were present, and evidently Morag felt Alison was sufficiently part of the family to continue bitterly as Hector moved away, 'Really, Jennie takes too much upon herself! Sometimes she seems to forget that even if I am only the *second* Mrs Heseltine, still I am Seaton's wife and know what is best for him, and I've told her time and again that I don't feel it's good for him to spend so much time alone in his room. He feels the better of social contacts, and I'm sure David's being with us would have cheered him up and taken his mind off himself and off the past for a little.'

Silence greeted this outburst. Alison was afraid to speak for fear of saying the wrong thing and there was a grim line about Keith's lips that boded no good to someone. Did Keith know of Jennie's habit of listening at doors? Alison wondered. But of course he did. And doubtless he resented the curiously proprietorial manner that Jennie assumed towards Seaton and to the whole Heseltine household.

Into the silence came the faint sound of a car beyond the thick walls. The sound of the engine ceased and shortly the big door was pushed open and David Inglis joined them.

His presence was a welcome addition to their little group, Alison decided; he seemed to merge effortlessly into the company as he accepted the drink which Hector brought. Even Morag seemed brighter and more self-confident in his presence, she noticed, as he complimented her on a rather pretty dress of dark red she was wearing: the deep colour helped to subdue the redness of her skin and gave her a glow that was becoming.

Alison herself felt that she was breathing more easily in the presence of this young man whose conversation and easy manner reminded her of the men she had been friendly with in England. For a moment she was reminded of Toby Benson and she shut her eyes tightly in a spasm of something like pain as the vivid image of his attentive face flashed across her mind for a moment.

There was a great resemblance between David and the irrepressible Simon: David had the same vivid blue eyes and broad forehead as his son, but his hair was dark instead of the carroty tone of Simon's.

'You're from England, I understand,' David's bright blue eyes held Alison's as soon as he could with politeness turn his attention from Morag. 'You know I spent almost five years there. I was on the staff of—'

But where David had been employed was something Alison was not to learn then. They were interrupted by the trilling cry, 'David! How simply wonderful of you to come!' and down the stairs glided a figure which at first Alison had a moment's dificulty in recognising as Hester's. She was dressed in what was evidently the contents of the blue and white box which she had borne so carefully out of the shop in Aberdeen, a stunning gown of black and green sequins, which clung to her perfect little figure. Her hair was piled high and interlaced with pearls and her face was elaborately made up. But as she drew near the effect produced was something like comedy as the undoubted youthfulness of her face and expression came into view. The general effect was ludicrous and Alison had as much as she could do to restrain a giggle.

She was conscious of Keith morosely regarding his sister. Morag caught her eye and raised her hands in a little gesture of helplessness as Hester swayed forward. 'Do fetch me a drink, David,' she said with an affectation of languid sophistication that was strikingly in contrast to her morose everyday manner.

'And what is it to be?' David asked, a gleam in his blue eyes. 'Orangeade, or would you prefer lime flavour?'

'Cut it out, David. I'm not a child and I won't be treated like one,' Hester said bellicosely with an abrupt transition to her normal manner.

'A grown-up drink,' David mused. 'Let me see, whisky, brandy, gin, vodka—'

An angry, youthful flush was clashing with Hester's elaborate make-up and she was about to burst into an angry response to this teasing when fortunately dinner was announced.

Hester ate in sulky silence during the early part of the meal, but when it became apparent that David was not perturbed by her attitude and that instead he was devoting his attention to Alison, Hester abruptly changed her attitude and exerted herself by every way she knew to attract his attention to her.

Afterwards, nothing would do her but she

would slip into his car and accompany him back to Correybrae.

'Really, Hester,' Morag protested in exasperation as she was about to depart, 'how can you walk back in that ridiculous dress? At least put on a warm coat.'

But this Hester scorned to do and with something like a sigh David acquiesced as Hester accompanied him across the hall after he had made his farewells, and they could hear him arguing with her before he eventually capitulated and they drove off together.

'I can do nothing with that stepdaughter of mine,' Morag lamented after their departure. 'I often wonder if I had been a different sort of woman would I have been more successful, or is it something in the Heseltines that would have overcome even the most determined sort of person.'

'It's something in the Heseltines, you may be sure,' Keith assured her grimly. 'There's a dark streak runs through the Heseltines' family, both men and women, which makes them uncomfortable people to know.'

Later, when they had dispersed to their rooms, this remark of Keith's remained in Alison's mind. She felt excited and wakeful. The events of the day seemed to spin through her head. She threw a warm coat over the light dress she had worn at dinner and stole downstairs. The great house was silent and deserted, the inhabitants had gone to their rooms while the servants were snug in their own quarters, possibly seated around a cosy fire, discussing the doings of the day.

Even the creaks of the treads in the old oak staircase were familiar. Vividly they brought back to her the days when she had sped silently down these stairs when she was only a girl and had lingered too late in the great house. Then she had flitted downstairs silently, avoiding those treads with their tell-tale creaks when she had hurried off to the cottage, late but still hoping to get back before her mother returned, tired after an exhausting day of companionship to Flora Heseltine.

Now she slipped back the bolts silently on a side door and moved out into the evening air. The night was gloomy and chill—mist rising from the lower ground and hanging over the surface of the lawn to the side of the house. Without thinking, she took the familiar path towards the cottage, where a little burn ran gushing swiftly over stony boulders. As she drew near she gave a gasp of dismay as she saw how dilapidated it had become in the years that had passed since she had left Abercorrey. The giant holly hedge, once clipped into a great dark block, had been neglected and now grew shapeless and looming over the windows to the side of the little house. The grasses stood high and rank in what had once been the tiny patch of lawn in which they had sat in deckchairs and sipped lemonade in those few fine summer afternoons when her mother had been free from her duties at the great house.

Slowly Alison put out her hand to the thick wooden handle of the door. It turned and she found herself standing once more in the tiny living-room. She was aware of, rather than saw, the familiar objects in the room, the chairs and sofa which her mother had covered with chintz, the dark wood of the clock on the white-painted mantelshelf, the thick white sheepskin rug before the fireplace, the cabinet in the corner, filled with the little objects that had fascinated her as a child, the shepherdess forever striding forwards, a straw hat on her head and a basket of flowers dangling from her elbow. The toby jugs with their thick black glaze, the willow pattern china, the long brass toasting fork, the ivory figurine of a fisherman with a net slung over his shoulder, the blue and white Chinese bowls and the long porcelain spoon.

Slowly she moved across the room and opened the door of the tiny room that had been hers. But the shutters seemed to be closed and she could discern nothing; and as she turned her head again towards the living-room she let out a strangled scream, for now a dark figure stood in the doorway, silhouetted dimly against the misty light outside.

'It's all right, don't be scared,' came Keith's deep tones. 'I saw someone slip into the cottage and came along to investigate, but I should have guessed it would be you.'

As he spoke he struck a match and holding it up surveyed her. 'You look as pale as a ghost,' he said abruptly. 'But then that is what you are, Alison, aren't you, a ghost from the past, unseasonably haunting us.'

As he spoke the match flickered and went out and her eyes followed the arc of the tiny red ember as he flung it towards the fireplace.

'What do you mean?' she asked in a voice that she recongised held a betraying quaver.

'You know only too well. Why are you here alone in the dark flitting about this spot if you're not trying to recapture the past?'

So he had seen through her return, she thought. She had indeed been trying to recapture the magic of youth when she had made that impulsive determined effort to flee away from Geralda, from Market Hanboury and Toby and the mess she had made of her life there.

And immediately there followed a moment of anger against Seaton. The reason for Keith's fury of rudeness when she had first met him that afternoon was now only too clear. He had known of his father's hope that in Alison his strange unpredictable son might find the only woman in the world capable of understanding him and of loving him in spite of his waywardness and all his faults.

Seaton's tactless attempt to throw them together had spoiled whatever chance there had ever been of their taking up their old friendship and of its growing into something more adult and satisfying.

Here before her was the one person in the world with whom she could have discussed the impulse that had made her steal down to the cottage trying to recapture the past.

Instead, she said in as matter-of-fact a voice as she could summon, 'I thought I'd take a look at the cottage, see what condition it was in after all these years.'

'Well, and what's your decision?' his voice came to her abruptly out of the darkness.

She did not pretend to misunderstand him. 'I don't thing I could bear to live here now,' she replied. 'It has too many memories.'

They went out together and he paused for a moment at the giant holly bush. 'Yes, things are changed,' he said. 'Even your window is hidden now; the hedge has grown against it. I don't suppose you remember it, but one night so many years ago I came here and threw pebbles up at your window, and when you came down I gave you a handful of rough cairngorms I had gathered in my wanderings. They were all about the same size and I promised to have them polished and—'

'Yes, you promised to have them made into

70

a bracelet for me,' she said softly.

'So you remember, but I didn't have it done, and now, of course, it's too late; you must have thrown those ugly hunks of stone away long ago.'

She longed to tell him that it was not too late; she had not thrown his boyish gift away. But since her conversation with Seaton this was no longer possible.

Silence lengthened between them.

'But of course you got rid of them long ago,' he said, taking her silence as confirmation. 'The cairngorms belong to the past, just as this cottage does, and that night when I stood here by the holly bush throwing up pebbles at your window. And one should never try to recover the past.'

In silence they returned to the house, but Alison felt that for those few moments in the cottage in the dark she had had a glimpse of the boy she had once known and loved.

CHAPTER FOUR

It was about a fortnight later that a letter came from Geralda containing news that quite shattered Alison. Already Geralda had tired of Toby and had decided not to marry him! But it was the final sentence that really stunned Alison, for Geralda actually asked if she might join her at the cottage for a short holiday—'to forget my latest indiscretion,' she had the nerve enough to add.

Alison tucked the letter into the pocket of her cardigan and set off for a walk while she pondered what reply to make to this incredible suggestion. First of all it was unthinkable that she should ask Seaton to put the cottage in repair so that she could invite a guest there, especailly as, not for the moment, did she wish to see Geralda again. She had suffered too much at her hands ever to wish to resume the friendship. Toby, as far as Geralda was concerned, might only be an incident in her life, but Alison's regard for him had been sincere and his betrayal of her with Geralda had bitten deeply into her self-confidence.

Her wanderings brought her near the busy little burn that ran past the cottage, and as she drew the letter from her pocket to peruse it once again a gust of wind plucked it from her fingers and she was forced to watch helplessly as the pale grey sheet of paper blew across the burn and came to rest for a moment in a gorse bush. Immediately she sprang across the burn, but her foot slipped on the muddy bank and she plunged knee-deep into the icy water. She dragged her feet out and waded towards the gorse bush, but as she reached for the letter it was caught once again by a gust of wind on which it was borne away across the countryside and disappeared out of view over a little brae in the heathery terrain.

She sat down on a great granite boulder, drew off her sodden shoes and stockings and was trying to dry her icy feet with a pocket handerkchief when, glancing up, she saw Keith striding over the brae towards her, perusing a slip of pale grey paper which she instantly recognised to be Geralda's letter. When he caught sight of her he stopped and raised his eyes from the writing.

'A nice cool morning for paddling in a Highland burn!' he remarked sardonically.

'I'd be obliged if you'd return my letter to me when you've quite finished reading it,' Alison said sharply.

Without bothering to answer he crumpled the sheet of paper, pushed it into his pocket, pulled out a large white handkerchief and proceeded to rub her feet, none too gently. When they were dry he tossed her stockings towards her and stood up.

'I'm not surprised you stumbled into the burn while perusing this highly interesting document,' he told her as he withdrew Geralda's letter from his pocket again.

'Give it to me!' Alison demanded.

But he stepped back teasingly out of her reach.

'I always read letters which I find floating over the moors towards me,' he told her.

'Why shouldn't I? I was walking along minding my own business when it flew right into my arms, you might say. And very interesting reading it makes too. I admire this Geralda. It seems from this letter that she's the lady who coolly walked off with your intended husband under your very nose and that she's now tired of him and wishes to join you at Abercorrey for a recuperative holiday. Frankly she sounds to me to be a brazen hussy, but then I've always admired brazen people; they're so much more interesting than the pale, wan types who allow their future husbands to be filched from before their very noses, only to be discarded shortly afterwards as being too dull and stuffy.'

'Give me my letter!' Alison cried fiercely, trying to snatch it from his hand.

But again he evaded her. 'No, not until I find out what you intend to do about this splendid young woman who regards the world as her oyster.'

'I shall do nothing whatsoever,' Alison snapped. 'The whole idea of her coming here is utterly ridiculous.'

'You mean because you aren't staying at the cottage?'

'You know perfectly well what I mean. It's simply that Geralda can't come here under any circumstances.'

But he went on as if she hadn't spoken, 'Because if it's lack of opportunity that's bothering you I see no reason why she shouldn't come to Abercorrey—or are you afraid to ask her in case she brings her fatal charm to play on David Inglis?'

'Oh, don't be so utterly ridiculous!' she cried. 'Why, I've only met David a few times; I hardly know him.'

'What of it?' he demanded. 'Don't romantic people like you believe in love at first sight? Certainly he appeared to fall for you from the word go, and made no attempt to hide it. Go on, I dare you to invite this Geralda. Ask her to stay here at Abercorrey. Her visit should be full of interest. I shall watch fascinated to see whether you permit her to snitch David Inglis from you quite as easily as you permitted her to take this Toby character. Or would you put up more of a fight for David, I wonder?'

'You're very much mistaken if you think you can force me to invite Geralda here,' Alison informed him coldly. 'I'm not a child any longer to be dared and coerced into doing stupid things I don't want to do, just because you want to see how they'll turn out.'

'Oh, very well, cowardy custard,' he remarked in mockery of the childish jibe. 'So with you it's a case of "once bitten, twice shy"!'

'It's not that,' she protested indignantly. 'It's just that there's no point in my meeting Geralda again. Things could never be the

75

same between us. But of course that's something I don't expect you could understand.'

She held out her hand imperiously and reluctantly he placed the letter in it. 'Oh, very well, if you insist, but it would have brightened my dull existence here in the heart of the Highlands to have observed a *femme fatale* at work.'

Really, Keith had turned into an impossible person, Alison was thinking angrily as tight-lipped she turned on her heel and strode back to the house her cheeks flushed as she recollected some of the more revealing passages in Geralda's letter. Not for worlds would she have had Keith know quite the extent of Toby's betrayal of her. Now by reading the letter he had placed himself in complete mastery of the whole situation.

She went into the library and sat down at the giant writing-table with its black leather inset and ornate silver inkpots. She reached for a sheet of the Abercorrey headed writing-paper and selected one of the old-fashioned steel-nibbed pens that lay in the rack before her. 'Dear Geralda,' she began, then hesitated, biting the tip of her pen uncertainly. In the silence of the library the busts of Cicero and Socrates stared blankly before them and while she hesitated, rejecting one opening after another, she realised that this letter was going to be much more difficult to compose than she had at first imagined.

In the silence the door handle clicked, then the door was softly and slowly pushed open and Tibbie's head appeared in the aperture. 'I do hope I'm not disturbing you,' she said, 'but I felt that it might be a good time to see my paintings. There's no one about, and we could go up to my quarters quite unobserved.'

Why they should have to chose a time when there was no one around to steal up to Tibbie's lair, Alison could not imagine, but this was probably a part of the old lady's passion for secrecy, she surmised. She was anything but anxious to avail herself of the invitation, but could think of no excuse and reluctantly followed Tibbie up flight after flight of stairs until they were on the top-most floor of the house. Here Tibbie opened a door and conducted her into what Alison realized was a vast attic. It was so large, Alison could only dimly make out the objects at the far end. The old lady had made herself comfortable with a vast four-poster bed belonging to a past age, and Alison noticed a chest of carved ebony that must have gone back to Tudor times and a vast array of massive Victorian pieces made of solid mahogany and carved with fruit and flowers.

Eagerly Tibbie led Alison to an easel upon which there was a stretcher holding white velvet. On it was painted a single gigantic red rose; the colours were vibrant and challenging and there was an energy and urgency about the work that impressed Alison.

As she praised it, Tibbie expanded. 'Oh, yes, it's an unusual art nowadays,' she informed Alison, 'but I believe it's coming back into fashion now that everything Victorian has become so popular. But believe me, the younger generation don't know how to set about it as I do. The technique is quite different from ordinary painting. You see, you don't simply apply the paint to the velvet. Instead you must make a stencil and then paint through on to the material. You dab it on, as it were, with a special short-haired brush so that the paint goes right into the velvet. Some people, of course, buy their stencils ready made in the shops, but I don't do that. No, every picture I make is mine completely—from start to finish. I think up my idea, make the design and then cut my own stencil. Actually this one is for the dominie. He loves old-fashioned things.' Eagerly she brought out one picture after another and displayed them. And more and more Alison was amazed at the talent displayed by this strange little woman.

On black velvet she had painted one of the wings of Abercorry against a sunset sky flaring lurid red through a rent in the clouds. Another subject was red deer against a background of mountain and forest. Finally

Tibbie brought out a picture that made Alison start back with a gasp of horror, for clearly depicted was the river Correy with its granite boulders and with spray flung upwards, and in the forefront, larger than life, a figure with fair hair falling forward, the face hidden, being stabbed by an arm holding a red-tipped dagger.

'It's good, isn't it?' Tibbie asked, regarding her with a curious eagerness in her round blue eyes. 'That's a picture of Ian's murder, you know.'

'But—but—' Alison found herself held hypnotically by Tibbie's fanatical stare, 'but Ian was drowned, he wasn't—'

'Wasn't stabbed in the back, you were going to say,' Tibbie finished. 'No, perhaps not, but that's what his murder amounted to: he was stabbed in the back by one whom he trusted.' Alison looked at the old lady in dismay. Did Tibbie really believe this or was she perhaps not quite sane? As if answering her unspoken query Tibbie continued, 'You see, I paint the truth, not just what happens day by day but the real hidden truth that sometimes people don't see for themselves. Ian was handsome and brilliant, witty and charming, and Keith always envied him and longed to have his place, and he killed his brother by daring him to swim across the river. It's just as I said, he killed him as surely as if he'd stabbed him.'

'But this is all nonsense!' Alison burst out. 'You're saying this because you liked Ian and you hate Keith.'

'But it's the truth, the real truth,' Tibbie insisted. 'I know everything that goes on in this house. Oh, they think I'm safely stored away up here in my attic, but I see and know more than they think.'

As she spoke her face was quite contorted with the energy of her passion and Alison listened in horrified silence as Tibbie in a torrent of words poured out her pent-up hatred of Keith.

Eventually Alison's attitude seemed to impinge on her and she drew to a halt. There was a long silence while she seemed to recover herself and then, with an abrupt assumption of her usual manner, she said almost coyly, 'But there, I'm keeping you from your letter. You mustn't let a garrulous old woman bore you with her old-fashioned pictures in which, I'm sure, you cannot have much interest.' As she spoke she was gathering up the paintings in a matter-of-fact manner. She picked up that horrifying painting of the arm with its red dagger and stacked it casually along with a painting of ferns and a spring scene full of yellow daffodils and forsythia.

And Alison, wondering if perhaps she might have dreamed that strange departure from Tibbie's usual manner, went downstairs in a bemused manner to continue her letter.

In the library once more she wrote a short, polite note to Geralda saying that as she was not staying at the cottage she could hardly invite her to stay there. She herself was only the guest of Seaton at Abercorrey, she informed her. However, if she were ever in Market Hanboury again, she was sure they could meet without recriminations.

She sealed her letter and then decided that she would post it right away. She went up to her room, slipped on a warm coat and set off for the village.

As she passed the gate of the old schoolhouse, David Inglis came out.

'Well, this is a pleasant surprise,' he greeted her. 'And how are you enjoying your stay at Abercorrey?'

He fell into step with her as she told him that she was on her way to post a letter and she found herself chatting to him with ease. It was wonderful to meet a calm, well-adjusted person like David, she was thinking; someone who was outside the dark passions that rent the house of Abercorrey. Impulsively she told him of Geralda, and in his silent attention to her story she felt that she could trust him.

'You're quite right not to entertain the idea of inviting this Geralda here,' David said gravely when she had finished her story. 'She seems to be an utterly treacherous person and you'd be foolish to have anything more to do with her.'

This so exactly echoed her own ideas that Alison was delighted to have his verdict. 'That's exactly what I've put in my letter,' she told him. 'Although Keith looks on it as cowardice. He says it must have been my own fault if I lost Toby and that I'm too cowardly to face up to the girl who won him from me.'

'I'm afraid Keith can be mischievous at times,' David said with a smile. 'He was probably teasing you.'

'Yes, I think that was it,' Alison agreed without conviction.

As she slipped the letter into the post box she felt reassured by her conversation with David that in giving Geralda a decisive refusal she was doing the right thing.

At tea that evening before the blazing fire in the hall Keith, for once, was present.

'Guess the latest,' he informed Alison as she joined them. 'Hester has discovered that all these years she has had a hidden talent for music. She had now decided to have lessons from Lowrie on the organ.'

'Now, Keith, don't tease the poor child,' Morag murmured absently, as she peered into the great fluted Georgian silver tea-pot and added water.

'What business is it of yours, Keith?' snapped Hester, her young face sullen.

'I greatly feel that David Inglis rather than organ music is the attraction drawing you to the schoolhouse,' Keith informed his sister.

'Oh, shut up!' snapped Hester. 'I'm sick of you sticking your oar into my affairs.'

'Now here's a girl who could warn you about the foolishness of your behaviour,' Keith continued unabashed. 'You tried to cling on to your boy-friend, didn't you, Alison, but Geralda won him in the end, only to throw him aside when she grew tired of him. Tell us, will you throw David aside when you've won him away from Hester?'

'What do you mean?' Hester snapped upright in her chair, spilling tea over the pale beige skirt she was wearing. 'Now look at what you've made me do!' she stormed at her brother, scrubbing energetically at the stain with a handkerchief.

'Surely it's quite obvious,' he said. 'Alison here, finding herself incarcerated in the wilds of the Highlands after the interest and excitement of life in England, is at a loss to know how to pass the time. The only personable young man in the neighbourhood is David Inglis, a visitor like herself. What have both of them to do but to pass the time as pleasantly as possible? The fact that you have an absurd infatuation for the unfortunate young man is hardly likely to be of much interest to her.'

While Hester spluttered something incoherent, Alison said, 'David is right: you are a mischief-maker, Keith.'

To her surprise she saw his expression

change. 'Don't tell me you're going to start quoting David at me,' he said in a cold, angry voice. 'This is what I hear all day long from Hester. David says this: David says that. David is always right. I'm sick of having David's words of wisdom flung at my head!'

'Now, children, do try to agree for a little,' Morag protested ineffectually. 'What is Alison going to think of us? She's used to civilised people who know how to pass a few pleasant moments at teatime, instead of fighting like savages.'

'Now that's just where you're wrong,' Keith told her. 'Alison is no pretty little London lady appalled by our savagery. Alison at heart is one of us—perhaps the most savage of us all under that quiet exterior, and for that reason I warn Hester. Beware of Alison. She'll take your man from you and throw him aside when she's tired of him. Mark my words!'

★ ★ ★

Alison was sorry she hadn't worded her letter to Geralda in stronger terms when, only a few mornings later after breakfast, she glanced through the window to see a great wide, white car which she instantly recognised as Geralda's stop outside in the gravelled space before the door and, a moment later, Geralda herself step out. As usual Geralda was a picture of perfection. She was wearing a suit of a fine, thin woollen material in a soft shade of green against which her fair hair, elaborately dressed, shone in the sun. Over her shoulders she was carelessly tossing a narrow blond mink stole and she wore a tiny cocky matching mink cap. On her lapel glittered a small delicately designed brooch of diamonds.

'And who's this fashion plate who's arriving?' Keith wondered, his eyes on that slender elegant figure standing outside in the sunlight.

'Why, it's Geralda!' Alison gasped. How dared she just turn up in this fashion, especially after the letter she had dispatched—or had there been time for her to receive it? Surely Geralda hadn't just set off for Scotland, assuming that she would be welcome.

'So this is the famous Geralda,' Keith said with interest, rising from his place and stolling towards the window. 'So you took my dare and invited her after all.'

'I certainly did nothing of the kind,' Alison said shortly. She glanced towards Morag and Seaton, who, for once, was present at breakfast. It was just like this new mischievous person that Keith had turned into to suggest that, without asking permission of her host or hostess, she had invited a guest to Abercorrey.

'I did no such thing!' Alison went on. 'I told you that I would write to her and—'

'Well, all I know is that we can't have this gorgeous creature standing on the doorstep.' Keith would not permit her to finish. He strode from the room.

'Your friend is very welcome,' Morag said mildly. 'But if only you had mentioned that she was coming—'

Alison could feel her cheeks burn with embarrassment and was grateful for the old-world courtesy with which Seaton broke in, 'Any friend of yours, Alison, is always welcome here. You know that. We look upon you as one of the family.'

Alison was grateful for this covering up of what would have been an intolerable liberty, but it didn't make her feel any more kindly towards Geralda as Keith led her into the room.

'You must forgive this intolerable intrusion at this time of the morning,' she trilled. 'But I'm motoring through the Highlands and I felt I simply couldn't pass without popping in for a moment to see dear Alison.'

Alison was aware for a moment of Hester's fixed admiring glance at Geralda's outfit before Seaton said with pointed courtesy, 'There is no need for apologies. Any friend of Alison's is always welcome.'

It was at this point that Geralda's eyes met Alison's and for an instant she got the curious impression that Geralda was startled and rather taken aback to see her there obviously completely at home in the midst of the family.

The explanation dawned on her as Geralda went on gushingly, 'I'm in such a rush, I'll only have time for a peep at that lovely cottage of yours which I'm simply dying to see before I must be on my way.'

Alison found herself giving a little involuntary gasp of annoyance as the full extent of Geralda's effrontery dawned on her. So Geralda had thought that she was safely tucked away in the cottage having her solitary breakfast, yet had boldly driven to the main door with the intention of gate-crashing her way into the Heseltine family under the pretext of being about to visit Alison.

'No, Alison's not staying at the cottage,' Seaton said with a note of dryness in his voice which was audible only to Alison and must have been quite imperceptible to one like Geralda who didn't know him. 'We are very fortunate to have her staying with us here in the house.'

So Seaton was aware of Geralda's gambit, Alison thought with mortification.

'Oh, in that case I'd better be on my way,' Geralda said with a quick little moue of disappointment. 'I've simply fallen in love with your lovely countryside. Is there anywhere more lovely in the world than

Scotland at this time of the year—and I must admit that I meant to simply throw myself on my knees to Alison and ask her to put me up in her dear little cottage, even if it meant sleeping on the floor.'

'There will be no need for that,' Seaton told her, again with a note of dryness. 'You're very welcome to stay here as long as you choose.'

'Yes, there's tons of room,' Hester breathed. Her youthfulness shone in her face as she eagerly devoured Geralda's svelte appearance. Geralda was exactly the kind of woman Hester hoped to grow into one day, Alison suddenly realized, and she was looking forward to having this exquisite creature here in the house for endless discussions of clothes and make-up.

'It's not often we see someone like you here in the wilds of the Highlands,' Keith said smoothly. 'Now that you're here we must hold on to you by hook or by crook.' He was gazing at Geralda with an interested, animated, admiring expression—an expression Alison realized that he had certainly never turned on her since her arrival—and impulsively she exclaimed, 'Did you not receive my letter telling you not to come?'

There was a stunned silence after this outburst and she was instantly aware of Seaton's disapproval of what he considered gross bad manners and Hester's basilisk glance as she feared that this sophisticated, interesting visitor might be summarily dismissed.

'Letter?' Geralda widened her amber eyes. 'But how could I have received it? Shortly after I wrote to you I set off on my travels—on an impulse. But then you know me, I'm all sudden impulses and really scatterbrained at heart, although I try to be so practical. Anyway, I simply knew you'd love to have me at your little cottage—to have a chat about everything.'

Alison looked at Geralda suspiciously. What on earth was Geralda up to? The idea of Geralda motoring alone through the Highlands admiring the magnificent scenery was all so much nonsense. No, whatever had brought Geralda to Correybrae it was not a desire to see the beauty of the countryside.

For an instant it struck her that Keith too had seen through this unlikely story as he said, 'If you really have fallen in love with the beauty of the Highlands what better spot to view it from than Abercorrey? Now that you're here we mustn't let you go.'

Hester eagerly seconded this and Seaton extended a gracious invitation. Alison felt mortified that Morag's welcome was only an unintelligible murmur, but of course as usual no one paid any attention to her wishes in the matter and, with a serene smile, Geralda slid easily into the role of honoured guest.

'I must get Jennie to fix a room for you,' Morag said quietly as she hurried off.

They drifted out into the hall. 'What a stunning outfit! I only wish I had clothes like that,' Hester said enviously.

Alison could hear Geralda's easy laugh as she said, 'No thanks to me. It would be strange if the proprietress of a boutique couldn't manage to dress herself well. After all, clothes are my business in life, you might say.'

'How perfectly wonderful!' came Hester's answer. 'You must give me a few hints, for I simply adore clothes and everything to do with fashion.'

'Actually this trip of mine is a sort of business journey,' Geralda replied. 'I'm travelling through the Highlands looking at your wonderful knitted garments and picking out some things for my little boutique.'

As she spoke she avoided Alison's eye. This was all a pure fabrication, Alison knew. Highland knitted garments were the very last thing that would go well in Geralda's boutique, and although Geralda was not an expert buyer she was far too shrewd to imagine that such a range of goods would, for one instant, be acceptable to her clients.

Just then Morag returned. 'I'll show you upstairs myself,' she told Geralda coldly. 'The housekeeper is busy at the moment, but we can add the final touches to your room later.'

There was a slightly higher colour than usual on Morag's cheeks as she led Geralda upstairs, and Alison thought with mortification that Jennie had probably been sullen and unco-operative when she knew that this new guest at Abercorrey was due to her own presence there.

'How sweet of you! I really do hope I'm not putting you out in any way,' Geralda was gushing as she mounted the great oak staircase with her hostess. 'My little overnight case is in the car.'

Suddenly Alison became conscious that she was standing at the foot of the stairs looking upwards at the slim retreating figure with an expression of annoyance, as Keith came up close to her and almost hissed in her ear, 'So now I see why you were so determined that this gorgeous creature shouldn't come to Abercorrey. The competition is far too much for you. Isn't that the reason for your reluctance? She outclasses you in every way. I bet you a million pounds to a penny that the story of poor Toby is going to be repeated.'

'And what do you mean by that remark?' Alison demanded.

'She took Toby from you with the greatest ease, and she will be here no time until she filches David Inglis. Naturally you're not welcoming her with open arms. He'll only have to glance at her to be knocked for a loop.'

'Why don't you mind your own business?' snapped Alison. Instantly, as she saw the grin that spread over his face, she regretted the childishness of the words. It was annoying to think that she had fallen once again into the immature spatting which they used to indulge in in former years. She had intended to be so adult and independent on this visit of hers, to show Keith that she was now a woman and that as far as she was concerned the past was over. Instead, she seemed to fall instantly for his needling—just as she used to do in their youth. 'Oh, shut up, you make me sick!' she burst out.

Instantly Keith burst into a roar of derisive laughter. 'Oh, come now, surely you're more grown up than that now,' he jeered, when he had recovered his breath.

Alison gazed at him, aware that she had an angry flush on her cheeks. Once again she had fallen into the traps he had been in the habit of laying for her years ago.

Without a word she turned from him and went upstairs. As she walked along one of the corridors she saw Morag come out of one of the rooms and close the door carefully behind her. There was an expression of resentment on her face that Alison felt was fully justified. This last piece of impertinence on Geralda's part was just too much, and as Morag, tight-lipped, moved away Alison determined to tackle Geralda at once.

She went along the corridor, tapped on the door and went in. There was no doubt from the appearance of the room that Geralda had already established herself. Tossed on the bed was her little mink cap and Geralda herself was standing by one of the windows brushing her hair. 'Just take a look at that view,' she said to Alison. 'All those dreary moors and mountains and rivers. It simply gives me the shivers. Give me Market Hanboury any day of the week—although for that matter Hanboury isn't my favourite spot on the map.'

Alison ignored this. 'I'd be interested to know just what made you decide to come here, Geralda?' she inquired in a cool, level voice.

Instantly Geralda's manner changed. She dropped the pose of the leisured lady touring the Highlands and there was the old sharpness with which she used frequently to address Alison as she replied crisply, '*You* should know why I'm here. I'm here because I can't manage The Gilt Cabinet on my own—as you must have known very well when you walked out on me. I've always been perfectly straight with you, Alison, and I've never pretended to be a good buyer myself. Almost everything I've bought since you left has been left on my hands. A few months more and I'll be forced to close up. I have my faults, but I've always been perfectly straight with you. I admit I can't manage on my own. I'm here to ask you to come back. You can return on your own terms. Ask whatever salary you wish—within reason—and I won't haggle over it. And you can run the place just as you choose and I won't interfere with any decisions you make.'

'It seems a remarkably generous offer,' Alison said dryly. 'Are you throwing Toby in as well?'

Geralda seemed slightly disconcerted by her attitude. 'Oh, don't be sour, Alison,' she protested. 'You know you never cared for Toby—not really!'

'Didn't I?' Alison retorted. 'And who are you to tell me who I am or aren't in love with? You've got your nerve, Geralda. Do you really expect me to return to Market Hanboury and meet Toby again, see him nearly every day of the week perhaps, after what has happened? Really, I don't know which of us would be more embarrassed. You've made fools of both of us and now you coolly arrive at Abercorrey and worm your way in here pretending to be a friend of mine. No, Geralda, I wouldn't go back again, not if you were to offer me a million pounds a year salary.'

Geralda's lips tightened. 'I'm not surprised you're not eager to go back to Market

94

Hanboury and dreary old Toby, not while you've that gorgeous hunk of man, that Keith Heseltine, within your orbit.'

Alison was silent for a moment as Geralda wandered over to the dressing-table and scrabbling in her handbag produced a lipstick and began to renew her make-up.

'Heavens, aren't I a wreck?' she exclaimed complacently, viewing her lovely reflection in the mirror. 'This rising at unearthly hours in the morning and motoring through the wilderness alone mile after mile is simply not my cup of tea.'

'You received my letter, didn't you, Geralda?' Alison put in coolly.

And equally coolly Geralda replied, 'Yes, of course I did. But as you should know, I'm not a person who believes in taking no for an answer.'

'Get out, Geralda,' Alison said. 'I'm not going to have you here—forcing your way in here pretending you're a friend of mine, when all the time—'

'And if I choose to stay just what can you do about it?' Geralda swung around from the mirror, a steely look in those amber eyes which could look so beguiling when she wished. 'The old man has made me welcome and that wonderful, fascinating Keith wants me to stay. As a matter of fact, I think without flattering myself that I've made quite an impression in that quarter already.'

'Then you don't intend to spend your time buying Highland goods while you're here,' Alison said, dryly.

'Can you imagine me going around buying Highland knits?' Geralda said with a laugh. 'Ghastly old hairy tweeds like that frightful skirt with the pleats the old man's wife was wearing.'

While she had been speaking there had been a tap on the door and Morag appeared in the doorway. Her face was flushed and there was an indignant glitter in her eyes. It was only too plain that Geralda's ringing tones had been overheard by her and that she bitterly resented the remark.

Geralda swung around with a tiny gasp of indrawn breath and for a moment the two women stared at each other across the room.

'I just looked in to see if you have everything you need,' Morag said with the stiff awkward manner that was habitual with her.

Already Geralda was recovering from her momentary embarrassment. 'Oh yes, I have everything. I think I'll just lie down for a little, I'm quite tired out with all the early rising I've done during this trip. It doesn't suit me at all.' As she spoke she slipped off her shoes and lay back upon the comfortable bed.

'Yes, I'm quite sure early rising wouldn't suit you,' Morag said with a pathetic attempt at an acid retort. It bounced off Geralda's imperviousness and Alison was glad of the excuse of leaving Geralda to enjoy her rest to slip from the room.

Somewhat to her surprise she found Morag hovering in the corridor, obviously with the intention of catching her as she came out. 'You don't want her here either, do you?' she began abruptly.

'No,' Alison admitted. 'As a matter of fact I wrote to her and told her not to come here.'

'And she didn't receive your letter?' Morag asked tentatively.

For a moment Alison gazed at Morag. Morag's harsh, weather-beaten features looked troubled and Alison wondered how much the older woman guessed. But what would be the use of admitting it to Morag?

'She told me she didn't get my letter,' she said evasively.

'I wish she hadn't come,' Morag said with what for her was a very positive manner. 'She's the kind of girl who's a troublemaker. She's the sort of person who sets one against another in a house. And I feel she'll be the worst possible influence on Hester. Hester is foolish enough already, goodness knows, what with her passion for clothes—she has run up fantastic bills in Aberdeen and Seaton will be positively furious when he finds out, as he's bound to do in the end. I can't cover up for her for ever. This girl will only encourage her, I'm afraid. Then there's her running after David. This girl is hardly likely to encourage her to be more sensible. Already she has made trouble between me and my husband. She had made me appear inhospitable, and as you know that's a great fault in his eyes. I only wish she hadn't been encouraged to stay—but then my wishes count for nothing in this house. Hester resents me and I have no contol over her. And as for Keith, while he's always perfectly polite to me, he's different and doesn't try to influence Hester in the right direction. All the same, since you came, things have improved greatly. Hester's not so antagonistic and you have been a civilising influence on Keith. But with the arrival of this girl things will change. She will bring trouble upon us, I feel sure of that.'

CHAPTER FIVE

Alison slipped a waterproof coat over her tweed suit. Really Keith had been right; it was no day to go walking in the heather, she decided, as she tied a scarf over her hair and picked up warm gloves. But she had stubbornly insisted on going and could not draw back now.

She ran downstairs into the hall to find

Geralda attired in one of the elegant outfits she always put on when she was going out with Keith. 'Really, how you can bear to appear like that!' she said, viewing Alison with something like disgust. 'You look perfectly dreadful.'

'Still, it's the right rig for striding through the heather,' Keith said as he joined them. 'However, if you're coming with us to Aberdeen I'll give you exactly ten minutes to change into something civilized.'

Come with them to Aberdeen, indeed! thought Alison. This was the sort of back-seat position she had been relegated to since Geralda's arrival! 'No, thank you,' she said stiffly. 'I'd far rather go for a walk.'

'But do look at the day,' he insisted, indicating the view through one of the windows where mist could be seen sweeping down from the mountains and blowing across the moors.

'Oh, let her go, Keith,' Geralda said with lazy contempt. 'She's probably anxious to get that marvellous misty rain on her cheeks; it's so good for the complexion.'

So it was that as Alison made her solitary way along the drive, her head lowered against the rain, Keith's big black car drove past, Geralda giving her a derisive wave as they sped out of sight around a bend.

As she turned off the road and walked along the little paths that led towards the distant hills she regretted her decision even more. The mist was still thick, but occasionally it would blow aside to give a view of mountain and loch. It was when she came to the height which overlooked a loch that the view was really terrifying. The mists parted to reveal the waters looking quite black in the murky light and from the edge of the loch a great eagle rose into the air with a scream and sailed off into the gloomy sky.

It was mere stubbornness which had got her into this pickle, Alison was thinking as she descended from her perch and began to retrace her steps towards Abercorrey. What had hurt her had been the fact that Keith had invited Geralda first, and it was only when she had agreed that the expedition had been definitely on. And it was then that he had turned to her and had asked her without particular enthusiasm to accompany them. She was mortified to remember that her rejection of the invitation had been rather indignant—to Geralda's amusement, she had been aware. Where was the cool, sophisticated Alison whom she had hoped to present during this visit to Abercorrey? These schoolgirlish scenes and her obvious awareness of being second-best in Keith's eyes must be highly gratifying to Geralda, she decided gloomily.

But it was all Keith's fault, she thought angrily as she strode down into the mists once more. Since Geralda's arrival he had given her all his attention. As far as she, Alison, was concerned she might hardly have existed.

As she walked on, heedless of the soggy dampness which now soaked her feet, a grouse rose almost before her, flew away with a whirr of wings and then planed off low over the heather into the mist. Alison quickened her steps.

It was as she regained the path that led towards Abercorrey that she was startled by a shape that seemed to move and weave somewhere on the path before her. She stopped, hesitating, and as she did so a little dog came crouching up towards her and licked her hand. It was perhaps the smallest collie dog she had ever seen, with a sharp little face and pointed ears. Its coat was wet and mudstained and the tail which should have been feathery was damp and bedraggled. He dragged one leg as he moved forward. 'Oh, you poor thing, are you lost?' Alison's heart went out to him and hearing the kind tone of her voice he licked her hand hopefully. He was not a pure-bred collie, she knew immediately, but was a mongrel of some sort, although he was mostly collie. He whimpered as he moved forward and she guessed that the injured leg was paining him. Picking him up in her arms, she walked back very slowly to Abercorrey and smuggled him up to her bedroom.

She placed him on the rug before the fireplace and kneeling down, put a light to the kindling which lay ready in the hearth.

Gratefully the little dog curled up before the warm blaze.

Now for something for him to eat, for he was as much hungry as cold, she guessed. She would sneak down to the kitchen and beg food from the cook, Mrs Fleming. She had been in the house when Alison had lived there formerly and was well disposed towards her.

When she entered the kitchen and told her story, the cook was all sympathy. 'It's not meat you should give the poor animal if it's starving,' Mrs Fleming told her. 'It should have warm milk.'

At her instructions Annie, the little kitchenmaid, put a saucepan on one of the shining stoves and set milk to warm.

This was the first time Alison had been in the kitchen regions of Abercorrey since her return and she marvelled at the changes that had occurred. The once stone-flagged floor was now tiled with bright squares of red and cream. The great cavernous range had been taken away and in its place were enamelled cookers embellished with innumberable dials. The ovens had glass doors, and modern work-surfaces made of hard, heat-resistant synthetics in bright colours replaced the great wooden table.

When Alison commented on the change

Mrs Fleming said with satisfaction, 'Aye, all Master Keith's doing. You could complain to Mr Seaton over and over again until you were blue in the face, but never a bit of notice he took. As long as the dishes went up to the table perfectly done and all his favourite foods were cooked, little he cared what we went through down here. But it's different days now, and so I tell Annie here over and over again.'

Smiling, Annie turned from one of the stoves with a bright enamelled saucepan in her hand and was just about to pour the warmed milk into a bowl when Jennie appeared on the scene, and looked about her enquiringly. Alison noted that Mrs Fleming, although she was many years Jennie's senior and had been at Abercorrey when Jennie was only a housemaid, hastened to make an explanation. 'Miss Alison has just brought in a poor wee doggie that she found lame and—'

'And just where it this dog?' Jennie demanded of Alison.

'Why, it's—it's in my room,' Alison found her voice falter as she met Jennie's intimidating eye.

'You mean in Mrs Flora Heseltine's room,' Jennie exclaimed in tones of outrage. 'You must know fine that's no place for a stray dog. You'll have to get rid of it, and that's that!'

'I'll do no such thing,' Alison retorted.

'Then I'd like to know what Mr Seaton will

have to say when he hears that you think no more of that room than to keep dogs in it,' Jennie told her ominously. 'Anyway, we've far too many dogs around the place. What with Mr Keith's prize collies that he thinks the world of and which have to be fed special, making extra work for the staff. Here, give me that.' She walked over and, with deliberation, took from Annie's hands the bowl of warm milk she had been holding, listening with bated breath to the altercation. 'I'll have no stray dogs fed in Mrs Heseltine's room, messing the carpet and leaving hairs all over the place, I can tell you!'

Alison could feel herself flush with rage. How dared Jennie treat her in this fashion! At the same time she knew that in objecting to having an outdoor dog like a collie in the room which was formerly Flora Heseltine's Jennie had a point. Collies were not lapdogs, and a bedroom such as Flora Heseltine's with its carpets and fine furnishings was the last place where one should be kept.

At the same time she had no intention of abandoning the poor animal which had already come to trust her. He must be fed no matter how deeply Jennie objected. 'Give me the milk,' she stormed at Jennie. 'He must be fed: I can't leave him to starve.'

But Jennie held on to the bowl of milk stubbornly, her small face set in an air of authority. And Alison was aware that the cook and the little kitchenmaid were watching with absorbed interest the outcome of the fracas. They sympathised with her, she knew, yet were afraid of drawing Jennie's wrath upon themselves by saying as much as a word in her defence.

It was Hector who came to her rescue. He came into the kitchen and stood behind them listening for a few moments, then broke in, 'Don't worry, Miss Alison, I'll take the wee dog of yours out to one of the stables. Dinnae fear, I'll take good care of it.'

Jennie swung round to confront him. 'You keep out of this, Hector. This is none of your business,' she informed him sharply.

Hector, however, seemed unimpressed by her imperious manner. 'Don't you try your bullying tricks on me, miss,' he rumbled ominously. 'I know a deal too much about you, so hold your tongue!'

To Alison's surprise the colour faded from Jennie's cheeks and she gave a sharp, almost defensive glance towards Cook and Annie. But she quickly recovered her poise. She drew herself upright and demanded, 'And just what do you mean by that remark, my good man?'

'Oh, never you mind,' he returned. 'And I'll thank you not to "my-good-man" me. Here, give me that milk.' He held out his hand peremptorily and Jennie, with an elaborate shrug of indifference, handed the

105

bowl to him.

'Oh, very well, then,' she snapped. 'But you can be sure I'll report this and you can face the music yourself. All I ask is that you get that dog out of the house quickly.'

'Thank you for your kind permission, madame,' Hector said with elaborate sarcasm. 'But that is exactly what I hae in mind to do.'

True to his word he carried down the little dog and ensconced it safely in a straw-filled manger in one of the stables which was not in use. He rubbed it down until its fur fluffed out and Alison gave it the warm milk which it lapped eagerly.

Hector stood back surveying it critically. 'I'd say yon's a bonnie dog after the sheep,' he pronounced at last. 'He's the look of a dog that would be fine at hirsel-running.'

'Hirsel-running?' Alison inquired.

Hector chuckled. 'I'd say that's double Dutch to you, but it means gathering the sheep from a distance, and it's not always a dog is good at that. Some of them excel at gathering the sheep around the bught—that's the fold, ye ken.'

'But how can you tell that, simply by looking at him?'

'By the cockit ears of him and the look of the eye. I tell you what, if he heals up we'll give him a bit of training and if it happens he shapes up nicely, we'll enter him for the sheepdog trials at the Correybrae Gathering.'

'Oh, would you, Hector?' Alison breathed. It would be wonderful to have her own dog in the sheepdog trials where such almost unbelievable feats of intelligence and co-operation between shepherd and dog were performed.

'Oh aye, I'd like to have a dog to train again,' Hector said. 'Although it's many a day since I herded sheep on the hills in the mist and the cold and now I'm long since past it. But still I have the patience to train a dog—and plenty of patience you need for it, too. Never a blow must be struck—that's a sure way to ruin a fine dog. But everything must be done with kindness and plenty of praise when the dog tries his best to please you and do your bidding.'

'So here you are!' David's voice spoke behind them. 'I was told at the house that you had brought home a stray dog and that I'd find you out here at the stables.' As he spoke his eyes fixed on the little dog, now curled around in the straw-filled manger. 'Don't tell me this is your new pet?' he asked, surprise in his voice.

'Oh, he doesn't look anything now,' Alison defended her new acquisition, 'but when his leg is healed and he's groomed and well fed you'll see a great difference.'

'Aye, you'll see a fine sheepdog if I'm not much mistaken,' Hector informed him.

'If his leg heals properly, Hector is going to

train him for me and we'll enter him for the sheepdog trials at the Correybrae Gathering,' Alison told him.

'That's a sort of fair, isn't it?' David said a little doubtfully. 'I've heard the event is in the offing. Prizes for the best pots of home-made jam and marmalade and the best knitted garment.'

'Aye, and the tossing of the caber and highland dancing; reels and strathspeys and the sword dance. Throwing the hammer—'

'And sheepdog trials,' Alison concluded.

'At which you fully expect this little animal to carry off all the prizes,' David laughed.

'Just you wait and see,' Alison told him.

'Well, I'm looking forward to this stirring event in Correybrae,' David smiled. 'I've never been at a gathering before, so it will all be new to me.'

As they turned out of the stable David said, 'What I called for was to ask you to come with me to help me choose a length of tweed for a suit for my mother. I suppose you know about the cottage industry which has been set up. I promised Lowrie I'd patronise it.'

'Why, I'd like that,' Alison told him.

She went up to her room, changed into a dress and threw a light, pale coat over her shoulders.

She was just turning into one of the main corridors when she was joined by Morag who came along from Seaton's room. Her face was flushed and there was an air of agitation about her that made Alison pause and look at her enquiringly.

'Really, Jennie takes far too much upon herself,' Morag said with what, for her, was surprising heat. 'She has persuaded Seaton to spend the rest of the day in his room, although I've told her time and again that I don't think it's good for him. He's far better in the library amongst his books where he can forget himself and his woes. And meeting people and mixing with the family, even if it is only for a meal, is refreshing for him. But Jennie ignores my wishes—as indeed so does everyone here at Abercorrey.'

Alison looked at her sympathetically. She had noticed how Morag's wishes were often flouted and had decided that it would have been better for Morag if she had insisted on her position in the house being acknowledged.

'It has been extremely difficult for me here, even from the time I was newly married,' Morag went on with rising anger. 'Hester was so resentful of me. I've tried and tried to make a friend of her, but all my efforts are useless. She's a selfish, self-centred girl, completely wrapped up in her own affairs, and seems to bear a grudge against me, simply because I married her father. Keith, on the other hand, has always shown me respect and consideration. If it weren't for him, I don't know how I could stand it. I'm saying these things to you, Alison, because I know I can trust you. You're discreet and don't make trouble.'

A little disconcerted by this outburst from someone as reserved as Morag, Alison said everything she could think of that might prove consoling, but secretly she was thinking that Morag would never maintain her position in the household until she exerted her authority—especially with Jennie. More than once she herself had found Jennie's insolence trying, and it must be much worse for Morag.

At first she had been puzzled by Jennie's position in the house, but had discovered that it was due to the fact that she was always discussing Ian with Seaton, constantly reminding him of little incidents in the life of the son he had loved so dearly—and incidentally putting in a deprecating word against Keith. The housekeeper, Alison had discovered, had a deep hatred for Keith, which seemed strange since he completely ignored her existence and never by word or look as much as acknowledged that she was alive.

As Alison slipped into the car beside David he said teasingly, 'I wonder if you're the right girl for the job. I've just been thinking that Geralda is the one I should have asked. She runs a boutique, doesn't she, so she must be very knowledgeable about clothes.'

110

Alison glanced at him fleetingly before replying in the same strain, but she was thinking, how like Geralda to pretend that the success of the boutique rested with her, whereas, as she had privately admitted to Alison, now that she was no longer there to do the buying and to oversee every detail of the little business, profits had fallen off. All that Geralda really knew was how to buy clothes that suited herself, how to appear elegant in the most trying circumstances, how to make a dramatic entrance, and ensure that every man's eyes in the room were riveted on her. Perhaps it was just that self-absorption which made her personal choice of clothes so successful but which mitigated against her ever being able to visualise what clothes would be suitable for other people.

However, to have said anything of this to David—considering Geralda's fabulous beauty—would merely have sounded like sour grapes and she merely answered lightly, 'Well, I'm afraid you'll have to do with second best.'

'You haven't seen our cottage industry yet, have you? It's been set up since your departure,' David remarked as they drove through Correybrae and turned off along a narrow road until they came to a group of cottages behind which was a small factory-like building. Here three girls sat at looms which made a clack-clack, clack-clack, clack-clack

111

sound as they worked.

'There are only three trained workers at present,' David told Alison, 'but Jamie here is having three more trained at the moment and hopes to expand the business if the venture prospers. And that's why you and I are here—to make it prosper at least to the extent of one suit length of tweed.'

Alison was looking around with interest. This, of course, was not the first time she had seen cloth being hand-woven, for she had always taken every opportunity to improve her knowledge of everything connected with cloths and their weaving or manufacture. But she was delighted with the quality and the wonderful feel and colour of these tweeds. In no time she was deep in discussion of colouring, which was by natural vegetable dyes, no harsh chemicals being permitted. This of course accounted for the wonderful soft tones of the cloths which seemed to spring out of the earth itself rather than to be artificially imposed on the yarn.

David was astonished to see the interest she took in everything connected with the work and how knowledgeable her question were. 'Well, I'm glad I settled on you instead of Geralda,' he joked. 'I'm perfectly sure she wouldn't have taken as much trouble as you have.'

'You must tell me what colouring your mother has,' Alison said.

'Well, she's young-looking and very pretty—at least I think so,' David told her. 'Although her hair is prematurely white, but she wears it tinted slight with a grey rinse.'

Alison studied the bolts of cloth. It was difficult to make a selection from the wonderful display of pink and browns, yellow and mauves. At length, after due deliberbation, she settled on a length of misty lilac-purple. 'I think perhaps this would suit her best,' she told him. When held up to the light the fabric was shaded like the distant Scottish mountains in the delicate lilac tone they assume in the evening light with shadows of blue like the deep Scottish lochs and a darker purple that hinted at the colours the hills assume in stormy weather.

When David had paid the smiling assistant and they went out to the car again a lengthening of shadows indicated that the short early autumn afternoon was soon to merge into twilight.

'I think we deserve some slight refreshment after our exertions,' David told her gravely. 'Now where's the nearest place we could get at least a cup of tea?'

'There are no tea shops or cafés dotted about in the wilderness,' Alison laughed. 'You're badly spoiled by living in England. The nearest café is in Aberdeen.'

'Then to Aberdeen we must go,' David said decisively.

Laughing, they piled into the car and drove off.

On arrival in Aberdeen they were just in time for the opening of a variety show at the Majestic and when David suggested they pay it a visit Alison eagerly agreed. They laughed and enjoyed the old corny jokes with which the comedian regaled them. The singing was excellent and when the show closed with an accordionist who led off the house in familiar well-loved Scottish songs, David and Alison joined in with gusto. 'The roses and the jessamine now grow upon the wa', How mony bonnie memories do they sweet floors reca',' roared David in as good an imitation of the Scottish accent as he could manage, which made Alison dissolve into giggles.

As they came out, Alison's eye was attracted by a figure slouching along in the slow stream of people drifting out into the autumn night.

To her surprise it proved to be Hester, looking unfamiliar in tight, rather grubby jeans, a turtle-necked jumper of dark royal blue, her hair scraped back and hanging in a tail on her shoulders. She was alone and on her face was a sultry and very disgruntled expression, as she chewed popcorn from a bag which she carried in her hand.

As her eyes met Alison's, then moved sharply to David, an expression of acute embarrassment crossed her face and she made

114

a compulsive but futile effort to conceal the bag of popcorn. It was clear that not for the world would she have wished David see her at that moment.

'Why, hello! And what are you doing here alone in Aberdeen at this hour of the night, child?' David greeted her, indicating the bag of popcorn.

'I'm not a child!' Hester flared. 'And why on earth shouldn't I be in Aberdeen at this time of the night—and alone too, especially when I see you've Alison to keep you company.'

There was something immensely irritating and at the same time touching about her brusqueness and her childish reaction to his greeting.

Really Hester could be the most irritating person in the world, Alison was thinking exasperatedly.

'Well, at least let us see you to your chariot,' David told her lightly, 'or did you walk from Correybrae?'

As they moved out on to the pavement Hester sullenly indicated the small, rather battered car which had become hers simply because no one else in the family wanted it.

'Now don't tell me you're going to drive back on that lonely road at this time of night?' David asked; the crowd had thinned as the theatre emptied and people sought their cars.

'I can follow you,' Hester replied. 'Or

would you rather I sat in with you—I can pick up the jalopy some other time—or perhaps two's company, three's none.'

Alison saw a shade of annoyance cross David's usually good-humoured face. 'There's no question of our returning at the moment,' he told her. 'We're having supper and—'

'And I'm certainly not invited,' Hester snapped.

'David, don't you think we should return now,' Alison said hastily. 'We could do as Hester suggested, have her follow us so at least she'd have help if anything happened to the car—' Doubtfully she eyed the ramshackle old car which she knew had a habit of breaking down at awkward moments. 'Or better still, could she not ride home with us and—'

'No,' David said decisively. 'I've no intention of returning to Correybrae early just because Hester is foolish enough to leave herself out on a limb like this by driving all this distance in a jalopy which she knows perfectly well is utterly unreliable.'

'Oh, very well!' Hester snapped, as she sprang into the driving seat and with a scowl through the window set off with a jerk that made the little car shudder from stem to stern.

CHAPTER SIX

Alison stood watching with a troubled face as the small car was driven furiously until it disappeared into Union Street. 'You know, Hester's right. We should go back now,' she urged. 'If we have supper now, we won't be home until all hours and—'

'And what?' David asked. 'You're not a child who has to be in by ten o'clock. Or is it perhaps that you're Cinderella and fear that as twelve strikes you'll lose your glass slipper and your clothes be turned to rags?'

As together they turned along towards Union Street in Hester's wake, Alison was thinking that it was true that there was no reason in the world, apart from concern for Hester, why she should bother to return to Abercorrey early. It was not in Seaton's cold, self-absorbed nature to care very much for any other living creature, and as for Keith and Geralda—well, they had each other. They would certainly not give a thought to her. David's interest in her and his pleasure in her company gave her a warm glow of reassurance as they turned into one of Aberdeen's leading hotels.

'Well, and how are you enjoying life at Abercorrey?' he asked as they settled themselves at a table in the spacious old-fashioned grill-room with its snowy damask tablecloths. 'Are you having a marvellous time?'

The question carried an ironic note that didn't surprise her, because she was aware that David himself was decidedly bored by his recuperative holiday in the heart of the Highlands. The society of his small son and his great-uncle was hardly likely to hold his interest for long, and Alison wondered how much longer David intended to remain on holiday. Without flattering herself, she was aware that her arrival had meant a lot to him in reconciling him to a holiday which otherwise would merely have been of therapeutic value.

However, this was not what struck her as she paused for a moment before replying. She was thinking that she had indeed been having a wonderful time—until Geralda's arrival. Now Keith and Geralda spent their days together—and Geralda showed no signs of intending to leave. She would drive off occasionally for the day, ostensibly to look at the hand-knitted jumpers and cardigans worked by the local women, but Alison was aware that Geralda's interest was in Keith. Keith was no Tobby Benson. She would certainly never be able to say that he bored her by his conventional and staid attitude in life. Alison, who seemed to have an especial sensitivity where anything connected with

118

Keith was concerned, had the uneasy feeling that at last, and rather to her surprise, Geralda had met a man who had really swept her off her feet, and whom she intended to pursue with tenacity.

But not for worlds would Alison have hinted anything of this to David. 'Oh, yes, I'm enjoying myself,' she replied, toying with the cutlery on the table. 'I simply love the Highlands at this time of the year. I go for long walks and—and—'

She paused and David smiled.

'In fact you go for walks in the heather. You'll have company soon in that new dog of yours. Have you thought of a name for the animal, by the way?'

'Yes, I'm going to call him Pride of Abercorrey,' Alison told him, stiffly defensive.

As she had half expected David threw his head back and burst out laughing. 'A grand name for a rather insignificant-looking animal,' he crowed.

'The reason I'm calling him that is because, if his leg heals well, we're going to train him for the sheepdog trials at the Correybrae Gathering,' Alison told him, with dignity.

'Really, that should be interesting,' David replied. 'I thought he was only a pet and to tell the truth he's not too presentable. A pretty little dachshund would be more suitable, surely, or perhaps a toy poodle?'

'Hector thinks he's a trained sheepdog,' Alison told him. 'He says he's probably good at hirsel-running—that's gathering the sheep when they're on the hills. Not every dog is good at that, you know. Some are really useful only when the sheep are near the bught—that's the fold. Hector used to be a shepherd at one time, you see, and had his own dogs then, who used to win prizes at the trials.'

David laughed. 'Well, I wish you luck—although it's a strange interest for a girl who has spent so much of her time in England. I'd laugh if your dog beat those of all those old hairy shepherds who are so proud of their animals.'

'I think Correy—that's what I'm calling him for short—is going to be a fine dog,' Alison told him. 'You can see right away that he's highly intelligent. And Hector's keen to train him. It must all be done by kindness, you know, combined with firmness, until he gets used to Hector as his new master. You must never strike a sheepdog. It only makes them cowardly and timid when they should be full of affection for their handler.'

'I've heard that,' David replied. 'Kindness with firmness seems to be the rule—and that's why no girl should be allowed to handle a sheepdog. It's impossible for a girl not to try to bring her dog into the house and make a pet of it, give it titbits from the table and generally spoil it.'

Alison sighed. Already she was fond enough of Correy to wish to give him titbits—but as to her trying to turn him into a lapdog—

'I'm afraid I shouldn't be allowed to spoil Correy even if I wanted to,' she told him. 'You may be sure Jennie wouldn't let me take him into the house. Even today, when I had only found him and he was cold and wet, she made us take him out to one of the stables.'

'That sounds like Jennie all right,' David said dryly. 'She certainly knows the importance of her position: is inclined to throw her weight around, I'm told.'

So even David, who was only a visitor in the district, was alive to Jennie's ways, Alison was thinking, her mind going back to Morag's impassioned complaint that very afternoon before she left the house.

'Jennie certainly keeps me very firmly in my place,' she told him, ruefully. 'But then, after all, I'm only a visitor and I suppose she remembers me from the days when I was hardly more than a child here and she was grown up. She doesn't seem to realize that the years have passed. However, it's none of my business, I suppose. Certainly I don't worry too much about her treatment of me. The person I pity is Morag. Where Morag is concerned, Jennie behaves abominably. She doesn't give her the deference which is

121

certainly due to her as Seaton's wife.'

'Why, what is Jennie up to now?'

'Well, her manner to Morag is far too domineering,' Alison replied, 'but that's not what Morag complains about. You see, Morag likes Seaton to get up and go about as much as possible, even if it's only coming down to dinner or moving from his room to the library so that he can browse amongst his books. But Jennie seems to be doing everything in her power to frustrate Morag's wishes, and the strange thing is that Seaton listens to her. She encourages him to stay in his room and to sink into the life of an invalid. It just shows you how much he has changed since I was here as a girl. In those days he would never have allowed Jennie to take the line with him that she does. I don't understand his attitude towards her. It's almost as if he were grateful to her—although that sounds a strange thing to say.'

'It's not so strange really,' David said slowly. 'From all I can gather from the village gossip Jennie has wound her way very adroitly into the position she has at present by playing on the old man's love for Ian. Morag wants him to forget as much as possible and to have other interests, while Jennie endears herself to him by constantly referring to Ian, repeating little anecdotes of his life and generally playing upon the old man's very natural sorrow for the loss of his son. There's a horrible irony too, about the position when you recollect just what part Jennie played in Ian's life.'

'What do you mean?'

'Oh, I'm referring in the nicest possible way to the affair, of course. Right under the old man's nose too! She's certainly a cool customer.'

Alison drew in her breath. 'You don't mean that you think that Ian and Jennie—'

'Don't tell me you didn't know?'

But it was plain from Alison's expression that this was news to her. It was true that Ian had always been secretive and the great majority of those who came within his orbit did not look beyond his charm and handsome face. But that he should have been conducting an underhand affair with one of the young maids in the house!

Seeing her expression David said quickly, 'Now I may be quite mistaken. After all, I'm only a visitor here and I'm merely repeating village gossip. On the other hand, the Inglis family have been so long in Correybrae that to some extent they look upon me as one of the family, as it were, and speak to me more freely than they would to someone who was really a stranger.'

'I'm sure you must be mistaken,' Alison insisted miserably.

'Very probably,' David said quickly. 'After all, I wasn't here during his lifetime and you may be sure people haven't spared his reputation. At least we should remember that Ian's not here to defend himself.'

But Alison, listening, knew that David was quite convinced of the truth of what he had asserted and she was aware that doubt was already taking root in her own mind. There flashed before her mind the picture of Ian accepting Tibbie Lochart's tip before her departures, with his charming smile and suitable protestations of gratitude, but when the big, old-fashioned car had departed for the station with Hector at the wheel, Ian had performed a clever parody of Tibbie's eccentric mannerisms. He had been incredibly two-faced, a devious and deep character, and she had to admit to herself that she had never understood him and could not truthfully say what he would or would not be capable of. All she knew was that there had been something in his character that had prevented her from falling under his spell as nearly everyone else did. Always she had preferred Keith with all his faults.

As they drove back to Correybrae the moon was up and bathed the countryside in a golden glow so that every view was filled with enchantment.

But the beauty of the night was lost upon Alison as her thoughts reverted to David's disturbing piece of gossip. Yes, it could quite likely be true, Alison was thinking, now that the first shock of the announcement was over. It fitted in with what she knew of Ian's sly ways. Keith, for all his rough and wild behaviour, had been open-hearted, an honest and staunch companion. In their own strange way they had always been wonderful friends in those far-off days of youth. But now things were different. The Keith she had come back to was quite a different person. Certainly he no longer cared for her. He was cultivating Geralda assiduously—and the strange thing was that she didn't even know if he was in earnest about Geralda. The generous, open-hearted, manly boy she had known had changed into an embittered, cynical, suspicious person, critical of others and harsh in his manner, capable of saying such wounding things. Oh yes, this new Keith, the man, was a totally different person from Keith the boy she had known.

The car drew to a stop with a spraying of gravel and Alison awoke from her reverie with a start. 'Why, we're back at Abercorrey already,' she exclaimed.

'Yes, and you haven't spoken a word for the last several miles. I really must have bored you dreadfully.'

'Oh no,' Alison protested, 'on the contrary, I've enjoyed today immensely.'

'Honest injun?' David said quickly. 'In that case we must do this again. I want to see something of the countryside while I'm here

125

and I can't imagine anyone I'd rather have as my conductor. I'm sure you know every brae and burn for miles around. Would you care to do that?'

There was an almost imperceptible pause before Alison replied. Suddenly she knew that she didn't really care whether she went out with David again or not. Fundamentally she had been bored in spite of the fact that his companionship was pleasant and she quite liked him. David had been right, her thoughts had not really been on him. She had been thinking of Keith even while she was in his company. She felt that David was a sincere person. He was, she suspected, cautiously looking out for a wife and she felt that should she encourage him, he would probably consider her in the light of a future bride. And yet—yet even in his company her thoughts had been firmly fixed on Keith.

Then, with a bitter momentary twist of her lips, she thought that in Geralda's company, Keith's thoughts had certainly not flown to her, and abruptly she said, 'Yes, David, I'd simply love that. We must have another day out together very soon.'

She waved to him before running up the steps to the house, and was aware of him sitting quietly behind the wheel watching her until she disappeared from sight.

Moonlight was sifting through her room as she undressed. Silence lay over the old house like a dark pall, but she found it difficult to sleep in the great half-tester bed. She was still turning and tossing when the door burst open and she rose on her elbow with a little scream of alarm to find Keith standing in the doorway, a shaft of moonlight striking on his dark saturnine features, and immediately she knew that for some reason or other he was deeply enraged.

'So at last you have decided to return,' he gritted. Immediately she felt her hackles rising. Why on earth should he take such a line with her?

'What do you mean?' she demanded.

'I mean that this is a fine time of night to return—and not even bother to let us know you were back. Now that you've got the whole household worried about you, you might at least have announced your return.'

'What business is it of yours what time I return?' she retorted. 'I'm not a child. I can come in at any time I please.'

'Not at Abercorrey, you don't. Not while I'm here,' he returned. 'Where have you been, anyway? Why didn't you come back when David suggested you should. At least he has more common sense than you have.'

'What on earth are you talking about?' she demanded, exasperated.

'Don't deny it,' he rasped. 'Hester told us all about it. David was anxious to come back with her, but you wouldn't have it.'

So this was another of Hester's distortions of the truth! In her overwhelming jealousy she had deliberately misrepresented the incident. It was typical of the girl's behaviour and for a moment Alison contemplated a dignified silence, but there was something about Keith's air of barely suppressed violence that forced her to justify herself.

'I see—so when Hester returned, she reported that it was my fault that we didn't come back earlier?'

'She most certainly did,' he replied grimly. 'According to her it was you who insisted on remaining in Aberdeen until all hours of the night. No doubt so that you could enjoy a long leisurely drive home with David in the moonlight while he whispered sweet nothings in your ear. Or did you, by any chance, run out of petrol? Don't tell me that you fell for that well-worn old gambit! Surely a girl with your experience of life should have seen through that one?'

Rage held her silent for a moment.

'So you did run out of petrol,' he mocked. 'My, my, what an opportunity for fancy-free David to indulge in a little romantic dalliance!'

'That's not true,' she blurted. 'It wasn't my fault we came home late. Hasn't it occurred to you that Hester, for her own reasons, had been distorting the truth, as usual?'

He was thoughtful for a moment, then said

in a quieter tone, 'Well, perhaps she has stretched the truth a little. I know from bitter experience that she isn't always reliable. Her highly emotional attitude towards situations tends to make her colour them somewhat. Sometimes I think she's not even aware when she's lying. However, I'm inclined to believe her this time, and I base my attitude on my knowledge of David Inglis. He's so prunes and prismy that, left to himself, he probably wouldn't have kept you out too late. He'd be all solicitous as to what the neighbours might think. Apart from that, he'd be much too cautious as far as he himself was concerned. Once bitten, twice shy.'

'And what exactly do you mean by that ambiguous remark?' she demanded.

'Aha, so curiosity concerning David has loosened your tongue, my girl!' As he spoke he strolled across to her dressing-table on which her enamelled silver trinket-box stood open where she had replaced the slender string of pearls she had worn with the conservative pale blue dress she had put on for her outing with David. He began to poke almost absently among the jewels with a thick, sturdy forefinger.

Alison jerked upright in her bed. 'Just what are you doing?' she demanded as she saw him bend over the box, a shadowy figure in the moonlight.

'Oh, just checking up on something,' he

129

replied almost absently. 'There's something I want to satisfy myself about.'

As he spoke he gathered something from the box and slid it into the palm of his hand.

From her position on the bed she could not see what he had purloined. 'Leave my things alone!' she exclaimed in exasperation as there was a clinking sound and it was plain that he was removing more than one item from the box.

'Oh, don't worry,' he replied. 'I'm taking nothing that doesn't belong to me. Believe me, I've no intention of robbing you of your trinkets. I'm merely repossessing myself of a few articles that once were mine in the days of auld lang syne. I'm amazed you've kept them all these years, considering they're of so little value. Not priceless diamonds or pearls of the Orient! Simply humble little products of the mountainside.'

'You're taking the cairngorms! But why, why? What are you going to do with them?'

'Never you mind,' he retorted with a parody of his earlier manner. As he spoke he placed them in his pocket and Alison could distinctly here the dull clinking sound as he jingled them with what she knew was a deliberate attempt to enrage her.

Alison could feel anger overwhelm her. How dared he come to her room at this hour of the night and coolly and deliberately extract the stones from her box without as much as a 'by-your-leave'! 'Put them back immediately!' she ordered. 'They're mine. You've no right to—'

'On the contrary, they're mine. I should have done this long ago. Before you left Abercorrey, in fact. You should have left them behind along with the part of you that belonged here amongst the braes and burns. Well, no matter, I'll find a better use for them. It's amazing how women are unable to see the gleam beneath the dross until it's revealed to them.'

It was an ambiguous remark, but she was much too angry to read any obscure meaning in it. 'You're going to have them polished and made into a bracelet for Geralda, isn't that it?'

She could see the moonlight slant on his swarthy features as he comtemplated her without replying.

Galvanised into action by such cool effrontery, she sprang out of bed and rushed on her bare feet across to the dressing-table and attacked him with something of the spirit with which they used to tussle as boy and girl when he had taken something she wanted. But now everything was different, she realized, as she tried to snatch the stones from his pocket. For a moment he held her off with an air of mock apprehension, then suddenly his arms relaxed and she found herself close to him, all the attack on her side. It was not like this their boy and girl struggles had resolved. Then it was he who was capable of resisting her wildcat rushes. Now she was conscious of her filmy nightgown, of his closeness, and, in an instant, before she realized his intention his arms were about her and he was kissing her.

For an instant she drew back with a little gasp, then melted into his arms. For a long moment he held her close and she was conscious of her heart beating wildly against the rough tweeds that held the subtle scents of moorland and bracken. A part of her told her that this wild embrace must not endure, but before she could break away the light was switched on and she swung round to find Geralda standing inside the room.

She looked extraordinarily beautiful in a filmy negligée of leaf brown trimmed with palest blue ribbon, and her look of bewilderment turned to anger as she contemplated them. 'Is this usually the way you greet each other?' she inquired acidly.

Keith surveyed her coolly. 'It occurred to me that Alison, after an interesting evening with David, might like to prolong the romantic mood.'

Alison drew back as though struck. He was saying in the plainest terms possible that his fierce and sudden embrace had been no more than a deliberate retaliation for her defiance of him.

Geralda, however, appeared not to perceive

the subtlety of his remark. Her eyes flashed dangerously.

'Indeed! Well, the next time you intend to indulge in romantic dalliance with another girl, Keith Heseltine, you might let me know. I've spent the most boring evening hanging about while you tramped up and down fuming as though you'd lost your ewe lamb.'

Keith swayed on his heels and surveyed her sardonically.

'You're mistaken, Geralda, not by any means my ewe lamb. Rather say my untameable wildcat.'

'Whatever she is to you, you appear to be on remarkably close terms. Just remember, I'm not the type of girl who hovers in the background while a man dallies in another woman's bedroom.'

'You're quite mistaken in my intention,' he said smoothly. 'Let's say I came here to claim something that belonged to me.'

'What do you mean by that?' Geralda asked suspiciously, her eyes travelling doubtfully from one to the other.

He shrugged. 'Make what you like of it, Geralda my dear.'

'I'd be interested to know just what's going on between you two. Just get this straight, Keith Heseltine, you'd better not try giving me the run-around. You and Alison, from all appearance, seem to be on remarkably good terms. Just how good, I'd be interested to

133

know, for believe me, I've no intention of hanging around waiting for your favours.'

'I suppose you know, Geralda, you look remarkably beautiful when you're angry,' he replied lightly. 'You should cultivate that emotion.'

For a moment Geralda stood speechless with anger and frustration, then, with a swirl of her diaphanous skirts, flaunted from the room.

Geralda's advent had in some way completely changed his mood and all his old mockery had returned.

As she departed, he turned to Alison with a grin. 'You'd better hop into bed,' he told her, 'before you catch your death of cold in that rig. I admit it's extremely becoming, but highly unseasonable.'

As he spoke Alison became aware that she was standing in the middle of the room in a filmy and revealing nightdress. With as much dignity as she could muster under the circumstances she crossed the room, got into bed and pulled the sheet up to her chin.

'I hope you're pleased with yourself— having a beautiful woman like Geralda fussing about you. It must certainly satisfy you ego!' she attacked.

'Yes, I admit I'm enjoying it,' he said coolly. 'It's a nice change for me, and I may say that in future I intend to have a lot more of this. For the rest of my life I visualise myself pursued by beautiful and enraged women.'

'Yah, yah, so you've turned into a breaker of hearts, have you?' jeered Alison, bursting into the scornful abuse that at one time had formed the mainstay of their conversations. 'Well, you can get out of my room now, if you're quite finished. I want to get some sleep tonight.'

He gave her the pleased grin that always crossed his face when he caught her out in these childish tantrums.

'On the contrary,' he drawled, drawing up a chair close to her bed, 'I want to have a little chat with you.'

'But I don't want to have a chat with *you*,' she retorted.

'Then why don't you try turning me out?' he taunted, mimicking her tones. 'But now, tell me confidentially, just between you and me, are you really in love with David? I feel sure the answer must be yes, because otherwise you certainly wouldn't go off for trips with him and stay out until all hours of the night. Surely you haven't become so careless of your fair name that you would do such things, unless you were passionately infatuated.'

He slouched back in the chair, cocked his head on one side, and regarded her with interest.

'Don't you dare try this line with me,'

Alison snapped. 'I remember you from the time when you were always tumbling into burns and never as much as had a heel in your socks. Don't try to play the sophisticated gentleman with me, because it won't wash.'

He ignored this outburst. 'The reason why I'm inquiring about your attitude towards David is solely for your own good. I'm warning you not to fall too deeply in love with him because for you the path of true love might not run as easily as you imagine. Women, you see, and doubtless you're no exception, regard a heartbroken man, not long a widower, as fair game: they're attracted to him like flies to a honeypot. But if I'm not mistaken you don't know the background to the story. You remember how curious you were about that remark of mine, "once bitten, twice shy". If you're still interested, I was referring to David's marriage.'

'What—what—' Alison faltered, and was suddenly conscious that she was leaning forward, her lips parted, as he said amusedly,

'Aha, I see that I've caught your interest at last. You're all agog to know more. Let's put it this way—David's marriage wasn't the idyll that Lowrie would like to have it. But for all I know, he may never have been told of the true circumstances concerning Sylvia Inglis's death. In many ways Lowrie is rather innocent, and David would be the last to disillusion him by telling him the truth.'

'What do you mean by that?'

'I mean that David and Sylvia were—how shall I put it—incompatible, let's say. The accident occurred when she was flying off to France for a week-end with her boyfriend. This was hushed up, of course, but it's taught David a lesson. He's wary now, although he gives the impression of being an easy-going and very uncomplicated person. He has learned that women are not to be trusted, so you can take my word for it that he won't be as easy to catch as you think. If you're only playing with him, take care that you don't burn your fingers: perhaps he's playing with you too, my girl.'

'Oh, do get out,' cried Alison, exasperated. Not for worlds would she have had let him know how uncomfortable and uneasy his words had made her.

'Now just a moment, my little termagant,' he interrupted mildly. 'I have a practical suggestion to make which will assist you in the predicament you've got yourself into. Before you spend any more long autumn evenings with this buttery Casanova you should put him to the test. Why don't you spend a similar late evening with me—oh, just to arouse his jealousy, of course. There's nothing like playing cat and mouse with a man to bring him up to scratch and to discover whether he's really smitten or not.

Tell you what, we're going deerstalking in a few days. You must make certain to be one of the party: it will freshen you up after the stuffy indoor life you've been living in overheated theatres and restaurants. We'll be out the whole day and come back as late as we possibly can—because I know how you hate early hours.'

'Come deerstalking!' Once more Alison pulled herself upright and flashed an indignant face at him. 'Well, that's one thing I'll certainly not do. I simply hate to see deer shot. They're so beautiful and graceful. They should roam around the hills free. I don't know how anyone could bear to shoot them. It's horrible and cruel, and David thinks so too.'

'So you're quoting David at me. David this and David that! You mean that David's not prepared to shoot deer himself,' he told her. 'He'd rather leave that nasty chore to others. You know perfectly well that if the herds were allowed to increase too much they'd eat us out of house and home. The herds must be culled and horrid brutes like myself are given the job. But like all women you're sentimental about animals. How you could love that ugly little dog of yours I don't know. If you're so fond of beauty that you can't bear to see a deer killed, how could you have picked a pet as unlovely as that Correy of yours?'

138

'Poor Correy is not as beautiful as your dogs,' flashed Alison, 'but he's worth six of them any day. He's brave and affectionate, and I'm sure he's a wonderful sheepdog.'

'Indeed,' he said. 'So if he's not beautiful, at least he's useful. I'm glad that there's something to be said in his favour.'

'Correy is a most intelligent animal,' she told him. 'Hector says he thinks he'll be good at hirsel-running.'

'And what may that be?' he queried, with mock interest.

'Oh, you know perfectly well,' she said crossly. 'It means he'll be wonderful at rounding up the sheep when they spread out on the hills—something that some—even some very good—animals don't excel in.'

'Dear me, you have become very knowledgeable about sheepdogs,' he said.

'You'll see,' she flashed. 'Correy will win the cup at the Correybrae Gathering.'

'I wish you every success, my dear shepherdess,' he said gravely. 'And now to come back to the subject near to my heart—and that is your spending the day with me out on the hills.'

Alison shook her head. 'Nothing on earth would persuade me. You're wasting your time.'

'Am I?' He tilted his chair back and considered her.

'Yes, you are! Now, once and for all, get

out of my room.'

He ignored this and continued to rock nonchalantly. 'Shall I tell you why you'll come?'

'I'm completely uninterested.'

'Will you be quite so uninterested if I inform you that if you persist in your refusal I shall be ungallant enough to inform your virtuous and conventional David how alluring you look in your extremely revealing nightgown. I imagine it would give him pause for thought.'

'You wouldn't!' she exclaimed apprehensively.

'Oh, but wouldn't I? Do you not know me well enough to realize that I usually carry out my threats?'

'It was true, of course. And the thought knocked all the wind out of her sails. In an effort to retrieve the situation she said witheringly, 'I'm flattered you've invited me. And what about Geralda during this long day on the hills? Is she to spend her time kicking her heels about Abercorrey?'

'But Geralda's coming, of course,' he told her. 'For one thing she'll enjoy it—besides, it will be educative for an English girl to see something of our sports and our way of life.'

'In that case, if you have Geralda present, you won't need me,' Alison said sourly.

'I don't deny that Geralda is a very fine person, almost flawless, one might say,' he told her. 'She has, however, one limitation. She never leaps out of bed in her nightgown when I'm around. In fact, beautiful as she is, in many ways she's not half as interesting as you are.'

'How dare you!' gasped Alison. 'If you think you can talk to me in this fashion—'

'Temper, temper, temper,' he chided as he stood up. I think I'll have to change your name to something more appropriate. How about Wee Willie Winkie?

"Wee Willie Winkie, running through the toon,
Up stairs, downstairs, in his nightgoon."'

Laughing, he went out and closed the door softly behind him.

CHAPTER SEVEN

As Alison went down to the hall on the morning of the stag hunt she found Keith coming in where he had been overseeing the loading of the station wagon. He was wearing tweeds with leather yoke-pieces that accentuated his broad-shouldered, stocky figure and air of strength and vitality. Hector was fussing about with guns and giving instructions to the stalkers and was generally in his element.

'Well, so you've decided to come after all,' Keith greeted her. He stood with his back to the fire and surveyed her critically. 'You're down nice and early too, and I'm glad to see that, because we expect a message at any moment that a stag has been sighted.' She glared at him sullenly, but he appeared unimpressed. 'After all, my girl, I'm doing this for your own good. You want to get as much fresh air as possible while you're with us, and spending the time sulking is not going to bring the roses to your cheeks.'

At that moment Hamish came in to say that there had been a message that a fine stag, at least nineteen stone, had been sighted on the hill. What part of the surrounding countryside 'on the hill' denoted, Alison could not tell, nor did she greatly care. A tremendous burst of activity followed this announcement. Guns were checked, the food hamper was thrust into the station wagon with scant ceremony.

Keith, returning from a trip to inspect the last-minute preparations, demanded impatiently, 'Hasn't Geralda made her appearance yet? She'd better come down within five minutes or we'll go without her. Do run upstairs, Alison, and find out what's keeping her.'

Without particular enthusiasm Alison went upstairs. Geralda must have slept late, she surmised. She was not sorry to think so: should Geralda back out, she herself might be let off on the pretext of keeping her company for the day.

But when she entered Geralda's room she found her standing in front of a long mirror surveying her appearance with every evidence of distaste. 'Of all the ghastly outfits!' she exclaimed. She was wearing tweeds and Alison immediately saw that they were anything but becoming. The thick fabric together with the ribbed stockings and brogue shoes she had donned did nothing for Geralda's blonde beauty.

Alison informed her that in any case a skirt and jacket was hardly the correct thing to wear for dearstalking.

While she was speaking Geralda pulled off the jacket with an abrupt gesture. 'Keith told me to wear "something suitable" and I've done my best to comply, but these ghastly mud-coloured tweeds don't seem to be my cup of tea,' she said petulantly.

'You'll have to wear something that will take lots of harsh treatment,' Alison informed her.

'Something like what you're wearing, I presume,' sneered Geralda, and Alison, catching a glimpse of herself in Geralda's long mirror, had to agree that even she had rarely looked so unalluring. She was wearing faded denim slacks and a very old turtle-necked jumper in a course highland knit with stout old shoes and woollen socks. Her hair she had simply combed back and tied with a ribbon because she was aware that no coiffure would last more than a few minutes in a day's deerstalking.

'How you could bear to appear like that is more than I can understand,' Geralda was saying as she fumbled in her wardrobe and drew out a trouser suit in navy blue and with white trimming and kipper tie. The fabric was thin and Alison immediately protested that it would be unsuitable.

'Keith said something sporting, and that's exactly what I'm wearing,' Geralda told her through gritted teeth as she changed into it. 'This is an outfit I wore for a yachting party and we were caught in a force four gale, so it should be tough enough for anything.'

Alison, aware that Geralda's temper—never the smoothest in the world—was at snapping point, gave up. Let Geralda face Keith in that rig, especially after keeping him waiting, and take the consequences.

'There, I'm wearing sneakers. Canvas shoes should be right if we've a lot of activity,' Geralda was saying as she tied the laces. 'Now I'm ready to face anything—and from the descriptions I've heard this promises to be a perfectly ghastly day.'

'But why are you doing it?' Alison asked. 'You could easily get out of it if you wanted to. And I'd say you'll simply hate it.'

'But of course I want to come,' Geralda said crossly.

'But why?' Alison insisted. 'If you hate the idea of the day so much why don't you just say you don't want to come?'

'And have Keith think that I'd never fit into Scottish country life? Not likely!'

Alison stared at her blankly. So Geralda wanted to give Keith the impression that she could easily take her place here at Abercorrey, taking a gay and easy part in all the various activities that made up the life here.

The implication was only too clear. To her surprise she felt a distinct qualm of jealousy and without stopping to think of the effect her words might have she said, 'You took Toby away from me and now you've set your sights for Keith, isn't that it?'

'What do you mean?' Geralda snapped. 'Keith isn't your exclusive property. Everyone here knows you're making a play for David Inglis.'

'It's just—just that Keith and I were always good friends and—and—'

She faltered to a halt as the thought struck her with sudden and devastating clarity that she was, in fact, in love with Keith. It was no longer even the memory of that boy and girl affair between them. Now it was with a strength and reality that seemed to strike at

145

the very roots of her being. Strange how she hadn't realized it until Geralda had spoken so openly of settling into the traditional activities of life at Abercorrey.

Alison's forebodings about Keith's reactions to Geralda's appearance were fully justified when they hurried down to the hall. They found him pacing up and down impatiently. He abruptly drew to a halt as his eyes fell upon Geralda.

'And just what do you mean by turning up in that extraordinary outfit?' he demanded of Geralda. 'Didn't you tell her what clothes to wear?' he turned to Alison.

For a moment Alison hesitated. But there was no way she could cover Geralda's faux pas as far as dress was concerned and she admitted that she had warned Geralda that her clothes were unsuitable. 'Well, you can just suffer,' Keith told Geralda. 'I'm not going to wait while you go upstairs and take another hour to change into something else.'

Without ceremony he hustled them out to the car and bundled them in and they drove off full tilt. The hamper was unceremoniously plumped down on the floor of a shieling about half-way up a hill and then the car was abandoned and they began to trek through the heather. Alison had brought a small pair of binoculars with her and with Hamish's help was able to make out the herd, amongst which was a particularly fine stag. The herd

146

was grazing peacefully on a hillside, unaware that now had begun a crawl of death aimed at their leader.

They set off in good spirits. Geralda's canvas shoes were light and flexible and she made good progress and kept up well. But as they drew nearer the herd they were instructed to crawl on their hands and knees and not on peril of their lives to raise their heads. Geralda, with all the good grace in the world, obeyed. But when they came to a stream and Keith and Hamish before them merely crawled right through, Geralda hesitated. She was on the point of getting to her feet when Alison plucked at her sleeve. The soles of her canvas shoes which had become damp slipped on the stones of the little stream and in an instant she splashed down, face forward, into the icy water. It was plain that she was about to give voice to her indignation as she struggled to her feet, but Alison managed to hush her. Hector also put in his admonition. 'Wheisht!' he hissed breathily. 'One cheep out of you and the stag's away!'

Geralda flashed him a basilisk glance, but she obeyed and crouched down on her knees again and the slow, painful climb recommenced. In a little while they were no longer permitted to proceed on hands and knees but must wriggle forward almost flat on their stomachs, and now Geralda looked a very different girl from the elegant figure who had set off that morning in her slender, svelte yachting outfit. Her canvas shoes were cut by the flinty stones, the knees of her slacks were split and her elaborate hairdo had tumbled down and lay lank and wet on her shoulders. Tears filled her eyes and she was sobbing and gasping for breath. 'I can't go on any further,' she moaned, her cheek against the ground as she saw ahead a particularly sharp ascent to the top of the little hill they were climbing.

This message, relayed to Keith, caused him to crawl back towards them. 'What on earth's the matter?' he hissed, his eyes on Geralda's tear-stained, muddy face.

I can't go on any further,' she gasped.

'Wheisht!' Hector admonished.

'I warned you not to come in those ridiculous clothes,' Keith whispered angrily. 'Well, all you can do is go back to the shieling and wait for us. You're obviously not fit to come any further.'

'And how am I to get back to the shieling? I don't even know where it is.' Geralda's attempt to reduce her wail to a whisper would have been funny, but for the fact that she was obviously in acute distress.

'I'll take her back,' Alison volunteered readily, glad of the chance to escape. He glanced at her sardonically, well aware of the reason for her eagerness, then nodded without any sign of gratitude, and in a

148

rebellious mood, Alison crept around in her tracks and began to crawl back along the route they had taken. Several times she had difficulty in restraining Geralda from getting to her feet and when eventually they came back again to the stream, she rebelled openly. 'If you think I'm going to crawl through that icy water on my hands and knees you're vastly mistaken!' she hissed in Alison's ear. She stood up and walked off along the little path towards the shieling, one corner of which was now visible, and with a shrug, Alison got to her feet and followed. As she did so she glanced around and high on the hill she could dimly discern the forms of Keith with Hector and a stalker. For an instant she saw the white blob of Hector's face and knew that he would be sure to report to Keith that they had gone off, making no attempt to conceal themselves. If the stag got away she and Geralda would be blamed. Although Geralda had been the culprit, there would have been no point in her continuing to crawl once Geralda had stood up.

Back at the shieling Alison started the fire from a pile of dried bracken beside the hearth and as soon as it crackled up put on the kettle. Then she raided the hamper for the makings of a sandwich for Geralda, who sat in a corner, her head in her hands, sobbing disconsolately.

She took the mug of hot tea Alison offered

to her and after a while she appeared to recover. Alison persuaded her to take off the muddy blouse and dry it before the fire, but the wide kipper tie which had quite made the garment was beyond repair, and with a revolted expression Geralda cut it off with one of the sharp skinning knives which were stacked in the hut and threw the wretched muddied object into the fire.

Meanwhile Alison was getting worried about the possible consequences of their standing up at the stream. If it had been the cause of the stag getting wind of the hunt, they could expect Keith and the stalkers back at any time in the very worst of moods.

She went out and trained her binoculars on the hill and was relieved to see dimly in the bracken the white blobs that spoke of the hunting party. Their bodies were visible as they wriggled forward on elbows and stomach amongst the bracken. They were nearing the top of the hill now from which they would be able to have a view over the nearby slope in which the deer were gazing and Alison knew that if she walked some distance along the track leading to the shieling she would have a view of the herd. She hurried along until the slope came in view, then once again trained her binoculars upon the spot where Hector had pointed out the stag. At first she could not see it and with a relieved bound of her heart she thought that it had escaped.

Perhaps some whiff of human scent blown back by a tiny gust of wind had been sufficient to warn it that men were plotting its destruction: or perhaps a tiny alien sound amongst the myriad sounds of the wilderness had been sufficient. But as she lifted her binoculars high she glimpsed it. It was lying down, its head raised, and only its antlers were visible, reared upright over the bracken. And now she could see the white blobs which were the faces of the stalkers creeping around the brow of the hill.

Then a figure stood up. She knew it was Keith by his proud, sturdy build. A second figure was handing him a gun. In a moment that lovely animal would be dead. Her heart sank. She was too far away to warn it to take to its heels and flee while there was still time. Then inspiration struck her. Sounds, she knew, carried strangely in that hilly region. If she were to scream really loudly would he hear her? It seemed utterly impossible, but she resolved to give it a try. She drew in her breath and gave the shrill 'coo-ee' that Keith and herself had used so often as boy and girl when one wished to summon the other from a distance, but her voice seemed small and pitifully weak in that great wilderness of hills and mountains. She watched the results of her efforts eagerly through the binoculars. For a second the deer remained motionless like a statue moulded in bronze and then, in a flash, it disappeared, and as it did she heard the faint echo of her own voice come back to her. The scream itself had not carried to the deer, but by some strange formation of the hills the echo had been borne to him, and that strange sound had been sufficient to make him take to his heels and flee.

Then came the glint of binoculars and she knew that the party on the hill had spotted her and that they must be aware of what she had done. Well, let them rage! She simply could not stand idle while that lovely animal was killed. Very slowly she began to retrace her footsteps towards the shieling. In a short while, for now there was no longer any need to crawl and proceed with caution, the party on the hill would return and then she would be in for trouble. Well, let them abuse her as much as they wished, she thought defiantly. She could not have done otherwise, feeling as she did about deerstalking.

When she returned to the shieling she was amazed to find that Geralda seemed to have recovered completely. She had re-donned the muddy blouse which was now dry, her hair had been combed and knotted high on her head and she was freshly made up.

'Where on earth have you been?' she greeted Alison. 'The men must be back soon. I thought I heard them shouting on the hill, so they must have shot the deer. They'll be ravenous when they come in. Tell me, where on earth does one find a tap where you can refill this kettle?'

'Oh, you don't need a tap here in the Highlands,' Alison assured her. 'You simply go outside the door and fill it from the nearest burn. The water tastes peaty, but it's perfectly wholesome.'

Jauntily, Geralda disappeared and shortly afterwards returned with a full kettle which she hung over the fire in quite an efficient manner, then proceeded to put out the contents of the hamper on the long, narrow table which was placed to one side of the hut. 'Venison pasties, I do believe,' she announced as she put out the goods from the hamper. 'How perfectly appropriate. I've never tasted venison in my life, so this should be a treat.'

'Well, I'd never eat venison pasties,' Alison told her sharply. 'Once you've seen a deer killed you couldn't face them again, and—'

'There's not much likelihood of your being offered venison pasties—not for a long time,' a voice broke in grimly, and Alison turned to find Keith standing in the doorway. 'That was a fine performance you put on, I must say. If I'd any knowledge of the limits you were prepared to go to, to protect the stag, I'd have made sure you didn't come along.'

'What on earth are you talking about?' Geralda asked.

'I'm talking about the stag escaping.'

'I hope you're not saying that it was my

fault that the wretched animal got away, but I simply couldn't face crawling any further through that stream on my hands and knees again, not if you were to rage at me till kingdom come,' Geralda told him.

'Oh, it wasnae your fault,' Hamish assured her. 'And after all, if it were, you're only English and know no better. No, it was Miss Alison, and I must say I'm heartily ashamed of her. It was her shout that warned the stag.'

'Well, you are secretive and sly!' Geralda turned to Alison. 'I did hear shouts and I thought the deer had been shot. Alison came in and didn't so much as pretend that it was she who had been doing all the yelling.'

'Never again,' Keith said grimly as he propped his gun in a corner of the hut, 'will I ever allow you to be within as much as fifty miles of a deer hunt.'

'You may be sure that I won't be there,' Alison flashed, 'and I wouldn't have been here today if you hadn't insisted and—'

She stopped as she saw Geralda's eyes go from her to Keith. Her angry retort had given away the fact that Keith had insisted on her presence and would only inflame Geralda's jealousy.

But Geralda did not pursue the point and turned away to the fireplace and began to make tea.

She gave this around with a cheerful word to the stalkers and Alison was amazed at her resilience. Gone was all trace of the fretful girl who had been scratched and torn by sharp stones, who had looked so bedraggled and tearful only a short time previously. She had made a wonderful recovery, Alison thought a little sourly, or was it simply the presence of male company that had restored her air of charming femininity?

Keith ate in silence, his face dark with rage. When he spoke at all it was to Hector or one of the stalkers and he was perfectly civil to Geralda. But for Alison he had nothing but stony silence.

His bad temper persisted during the drive home and Alison felt a curious sense of guilt, although she knew that at heart she didn't in the slightest regret being the cause of the stag escaping.

Her preoccupation with the thought that she had been the cause of spoiling Keith's pleasure in the hunt was quite swept away as the cars drew up outside the house and they were greeted by Sandy, the gardener's son, who had carried up her cases on the first evening she had arrived. His usually bright merry face was crestfallen and his manner apprehensive of a rebuke as he blurted out that Correy was missing. 'He darted away from me when I was feeding him,' he excused himself. 'I felt sure he would have followed you, being so keen on Miss Alison. You didn't see him on the hill, did you? He streaked off in that direction,' he added hopefully.

'No, we didna,' Hector growled. 'Why didna you keep your eye on him?' He began angrily to harangue the luckless boy.

'There's no use in blaming Sandy,' Alison put in quickly. 'Correy very likely did come after us and all we can do is look for him. I suppose I could borrow one of the cars.' She turned to Keith, her concern for his antagonism towards her quite swallowed up in this fresh disaster.

'You certainly won't go,' Keith told her grimly. 'How on earth are you to find your way about the hills in search of a dog at this time of the evening? In no time it will be dark. No, Hector and I will go, but I must say I'm heartily sick of you—what with ruining the hunt, and now your miserable little mongrel dog missing! I must say you've certainly done a good job of mucking up the day.'

'If that's the way you feel about it I'll search for Correy myself,' Alison said indignantly.

'I've already told you you'll do nothing of the kind. In another hour it will be dark and you, in all probability, will manage to get lost as well. Then we'll have the trouble of sending out a search party for you too. Go into the house and Hector and I will look for him.'

'But, Keith, why should you go looking for the wretched animal?' Geralda protested peevishly. 'We're all completely exhausted, and after all, it's not as if he were a thoroughbred and of any value. Anyway, he'll probably find his way back. That type of mongrel is hard to get rid of. I expect he'll turn up again like a bad penny.'

There was a moment's silence after this speech from Geralda. Keith looked at her fixedly, then, as though excusing her on the grounds that she was exhausted, he said mildly, 'Well, horrible as he is—and I agree with you there—still he's Alison's pet and must be found.'

And before Geralda could offer any further protests he got into one of the cars and with Hector beside him, swept off in a spray of scattered gravel.

Alison was pacing up and down the hall waiting for Keith and Hector to return when the door eased open and Hester slid in, a sly secretive look on her face. Under her arm were sheets of music.

'Hello,' she greeted Alison ungraciously. 'You still here!'

'Yes, Correy's lost and Keith has gone to look for him.'

'Oh, too bad,' Hester said indifferently, 'but after all, what's one dog more or less? This place is full of them already.'

She seemed wrapped up in some blissful

thought of her own as dreamily she laid her music on a table. 'I've been having a music lesson and Lowrie says I'm coming on very well,' she informed Alison. She drew a deep breath and continued, 'He says he thinks I'll probably be an outstanding pupil and be quite famous.' Here she stared directly into Alison's eyes in the fashion she used to adopt as a child when she was drawing on her imagination.

'He said nothing of the kind, I'm perfectly sure,' Alison said, irritated at Hester's obvious lack of interest in Correy's fate. 'You're just making the whole thing up—as you made up about my wanting to stay late in Aberdeen the evening David and I were there.'

'Did I say that?' Hester asked, widening her eyes. 'Well, if I did I've forgotten all about it. I don't know what you're making such a fuss about.'

Alison gazed at her in exasperation. She knew that there was no use in arguing with Hester. To this strange girl truth and falsehood were only something to be shuffled around to suit her mood of the moment.

'Anyway,' Hester went on, her habitual sullen expression deepening, 'whatever I said was perfectly justified. You're trying to take David away from me and I'm not going to let you. You think I'm only a child and that I don't really feel anything, but you're wrong. I love David. He is the one great passion of my life and if I can't marry him I shall die—or commit suicide—or something—'

Alison gazed at her in exasperation. How annoying Hester could be when she indulged in these histrionic scenes!

'And what's more,' Hester went on as she trailed across the hall and paused a moment at the foot of the stairs, 'I intend to get rid of you by hook or by crook. I'm not going to let you ruin my life if I can help it. I'll have you sent away from Abercorrey—just you see if I don't!'

In silent annoyance Alison watched as the slim, rather childish figure trailed up the stairs and disappeared into the shadows of the corridors above, with that secret smile still playing around her lips.

Alison paced up and down restlessly, but still there was no sign of Keith and Hector returning. Then it struck her that Keith would probably be in an extremely bad temper when he did get back and suddenly, unnerved at the thought of facing his wrath again, she turned tail and went off to her room.

She had fallen into a troubled sleep when there came at her window a familiar but long-forgotten sound. She jerked upright in bed as pebbles rattled against the glass. She ran over to the window and flung it open. There below stood Keith, and immediately she was relieved to see that he appeared to be in great good humour. 'Hello there, we've found your wonder dog,' he informed her. 'And what do you want me to do with it, now that it's back?

At his feet crouched Correy, looking even less presentable than usual.

'Whatever his faults, he's a faithful beastie,' Keith went on. 'He followed you right enough: we found him skulking around on the hillside.'

Full of compunction, Alison thanked him profusely. The day, as far as he was concerned, had been a complete disaster, yet, in spite of the fact that he had nothing but contempt for poor Correy, he had insisted, weary as he must have been, on setting out in search of him.

A pale watery moon was throwing a dim light over the grounds and as she tried to express something of her gratitude, she saw the familiar sardonic smile quirk at the corners of his lips.

'What's come over my little spitfire? Why, you sound positively lamblike. Well, at least it's made my efforts worthwhile to know that the return of the Pride of Abercorrey has wrought such a transformation.' He was silent for a moment, then added thoughtfully, 'I suppose the reason I went after the wretched animal was because, strange as it may seem to you, I wasn't altogether pleased with myself this afternoon.'

'You mean about losing the stag? she ventured.

'I mean about laying into you with such vigour. I should have remembered.'

'Remembered what?'

'Remembered the old days when you'd leave out porridge for the grouse. You were always crazy about animals, weren't you? You could never stand to see an animal harshly treated, or neglected. You couldn't help what you did today, no more than you could have abandoned poor old Correy here on the hillside.'

Alison drew in her breath, almost fearful that the thrill of pleasure his words gave her would be dissipated if she spoke.

'Then you're not too angry—I mean about today?' she ventured at last.

He shook his head. 'You've a soft heart, Alison. Always had and always will have, drat you. And now, I'll put this disreputable pooch back into his cosy quarters and get me off to bed. Tomorrow I'll have a word with young Sandy about keeping a closer eye on him, for I'd say this pet of yours would try the same trick again if he got the chance.'

He disappeared from view, whistling, and Alison returned to bed with a smile on her lips. She knew now that it mattered tremendously to her that he shouldn't be angry with her. She really had returned to

Abercorrey to find out if she was still in love with Keith, she told herself. Well, now she knew—but there was also Geralda, beautiful and practised in all the ways of attracting a man, and Keith had made no secret of the fact that he admired her. Suppose—just suppose Geralda hadn't elected to visit the Highlands—just suppose Keith and herself were here alone! For a long moment she let her mind dwell on the thought, then dismissed it with a sigh. Geralda was here, an established fact, and in all probability Keith was in love with her. In a man so enigmatic it was impossible to gauge his feelings. She herself would have to be content with such crumbs of his attention as were left over.

CHAPTER EIGHT

Alison was walking along the broad path that ran beside the river. Ahead ran Correy, his plumy tail wagging joyfully in the breeze. He had certainly turned into a very attractive little dog, Alison was thinking contentedly. True, he was small in comparison to a pure-bred collie, but his lameness had completely disappeared and since he had been well fed and cared for he had blossomed into a faithful and affectionate companion.

He raced back, weaved circles around her

and then darted off again, and Alison saw a weird little figure advancing upon her rapidly from the direction of Correybrae. It was Tibbie: even at that distance she could not mistake that diminutive figure with its curious swift, scuttling gait. She was dressed in long draperies and an elaborate hat over which she had tied a mauve veil besprinkled with large white dots. This was her usual costume on the rare occasions when she ventured outdoors. Alison had often wondered where Tibbie procured such fantastic outfits and had decided she rummaged in the attics and disinterred remnants of long past generations of Heseltines.

Before Tibbie made up on her Alison had approached the spot in the river where there was a great flat-topped rock from which the expert swimmers amongst the village boys were accustomed to dive into the great deep pool which lay immediately beneath it.

Even in summer only the most courageous dared attempt this, but now, at this late season of the year when winter was nearly upon the Highlands, the river had already increased in volume and flowed with a sullen roar that rose as it struck against that gigantic boulder and flung up a great gust of spray.

As she turned away, Tibbie came up close to her and said in an insinuating manner, 'I see you're looking at the spot where Ian was drowned.'

Alison drew back with a little involuntary gasp of repulsion. There was something pitiable about Tibbie in her strangeness and oddity, but at the same time Alison knew that she could never really like the little woman. There was a curious feverish eagerness in her manner and in her hurried speech with its unpleasantly confidential tones that repelled her.

'I wasn't thinking of that,' she said defensively. 'I was merely looking at the spray flying up and thinking how beautiful and wild it is.'

Tibbie ignored this. 'Ian was so wonderful, so talented that people expected him to excel in everything. It was natural that the girls in the district should have been delighted if he took the slightest notice of them. Not that Ian was proud or stand-offish! On the contrary, he responded to the admiration he received. He was almost pushed into doing irresponsible things, just to live up to the image people had of him.

'Look,' Tibbie pointed towards the house, 'there's Flora's room. You know, from one of the windows in that room you have an excellent view of this spot.'

'I know that,' Alison said a little sharply.

'Oh, yes, I had forgotten,' Tibbie said unconvincingly. 'You have that room. Quite an honour, surely. Now I wonder why Seaton directed that it was to be given to you?'

Alison glanced down at the little woman suspiciously. How much did Tibbie know? Surely it was impossible that she could have got word of that secret conversation Alison had had with Seaton on the first evening of her arrival when he had hinted so very plainly that in her he thought he had found the one girl who might understand that complex second son of his and care for him enough to marry him. It was true that Jennie had very probably overheard enough of the conversation from her vantage point at the keyhole to guess the purport of their conversation. But would Jennie divulge her discoveries to Tibbie? Surely not. Yet there was a knowing half-smile on Tibbie's diminutive face that made Alison feel uncomfortable.

'I was standing with Flora at that window one afternoon,' Tibbie went on, 'when we saw Ian come along this very path with a girl. It was here they stopped to kiss and Flora asked me who the girl was. She was always very short-sighted, you know, whereas I have eyes like a hawk. Well, I didn't tell her. It wouldn't have done, you see, because Flora was always a snob. She would only have reproved Ian—and he was entitled to his bit of fun, you understand. But there's no harm in telling you now, after all this time. I'm sure you'll be very surprised to know who she was?'

Tibbie's hints as to the identity of the girl with Ian made the truth only too plain to Alison. The girl the snobbish Flora would have disapproved of could be no other than the young maid in the house—Jennie. 'It was Jennie, wasn't it?' she said.

A shade of annoyance wiped out the eager malicious expression in Tibbie's face. 'How did you know?' she asked crossly.

'It seems there's gossip in the village about his "friendship" with Jennie,' Alison told her quietly.

'And why shouldn't he have amused himself with Jennie if he wanted to?' Tibbie flared. 'Ian was like a god; splendid and above the ordinary rules that hedge in little people: he had a right to his pleasures. And I for one would not gainsay him. I'm an artist. I'm broadminded: whereas, at heart, the Heseltines are petty, niggling little people. Jennie was a very pretty girl when she was young, as perhaps you remember, but more than that, she was full of high spirits and love of life, while he was bored here in the country. Ian was a boy who needed women around him. He needed admiration. It was his due. But Flora wanted to keep him at home. She didn't see that he needed a larger life than Abercorrey could give him. The secret had to be kept because Flora would have dismissed Jennie on the spot had it come

166

to her ears. I've never held it against Jennie. Live and let live is what I say, and I feel that the family owe her a debt of gratitude because of what she was to Ian.'

Alison could not view the matter in this light. She felt that the knowledge had caused the villagers to snigger, to them it would have been a subject for sly gossip and knowing winks. So David had been right when he had recounted the rumours concerning Ian and Jennie!

'You're looking quite shocked,' Tibbie told her sharply. 'You're straightlaced and narrow, like Flora. I could never like her because it was her fault I wasn't staying at Abercorrey in those days. Seaton would have had me. Not that he really likes me, but he has great family feeling and I believe he would have had me live here then, but Flora never hid her dislike of me and it meant that I could come only for short visits. However, Flora suffered for her antagonism: had she made friends with me I could have told her many things and perhaps between us we might have been able to avert the ultimate tragedy. I could have warned her to beware of Keith's jealousy of his brother, of the hatred that was growing secretly until it showed itself in what was no more or less than murder, when he lured Ian to swim in the river at that late time of the year.'

She spoke with such conviction that Alison

felt a sinking of her heart. Then she remembered the horrifying picture Tibbie had painted of the hand striking Ian in the back and her insistence that this was the real truth of his death, and as she gazed into Tibbie's round fanatical eyes, she wondered just how much of what the old lady said could be believed.

'I knew what was going on, you see,' Tibbie insisted. 'But Flora could never bring herself to confide in me, and in the end she suffered for it. It was her fault that Ian died as he did: she had only herself to blame.'

There was much more in the same strain, so that Alison was relieved when at last Tibbie broke off in her fulminations and made off along the broad riverside path with her curious, swift spider-like gait, leaving Alison to continue her walk in a very thoughtful mood.

The beauty of the late autumn afternoon was quite overshadowed by Tibbie's revelations. It just confirmed what she had heard from David in Aberdeen and which she had tried to tell herself was a malicious fabrication of gossiping villagers, but now she no longer doubted it. No wonder Jennie had that curious air of sly triumph! Even now, years after the event, she still held her position in the house because of Ian. She had insinuated herself into Seaton's good graces by her air of respectful devotion to his dead son. But just how serious had Jennie's affair with Ian been? Had it been no more than the sort of flirtatious association which the son of the house might have with a pretty maid? Or had it been something more serious—the sort of situation which his mother would have detested and done everything in her power to bring to an end had she known of it!

As she drew near the church, Alison could hear the strains of the organ, handfuls of discordant notes, pauses, then stumbling replays of phrase after phrase. The player was obviously a beginner and Alison had no doubt that Hester was having a lesson.

As she passed the tiny wicket gate of the small, stone-built house which was the old dominie's, David came out, a large bread-saw in his hand and a worried expression on his face. 'I spotted you passing by,' he began, 'and I wonder if you would have time to help in a domestic crisis.'

'What is it?' Alison asked, viewing the bread-saw which he was waving energetically as he spoke.

'Our housekeeper is away at present visiting her sister who is ill and I'm trying to rustle up tea for the family all on my own. My great-uncle is more knowledgeable around the house than I am, but he's busy giving a lesson to Hester.'

As he spoke he paused and for a few moments they stood listening to the

169

discordant sounds coming from the kirk. Each time a phrase was played over there seemed to be some new error. 'There's something familiar about that tune,' David muttered, 'but somehow I can't recognise it—not the way Hester's playing it, anyway.'

They went into the house and into the kitchen where they found Simon kneeling precariously on a high stool near the tall old-fashioned dresser. In his hands was a large tin of salmon and a pointed, old-fashioned tin-opener. As they came in he made a lunge at the tin with the opener: it slipped across the surface and he missed cutting his hand by a fraction of an inch. David sprang across the floor and seized the opener from his son's hand. 'Give that to me! Really, you couldn't watch that child,' he protested.

'You can stay to tea if you like,' Simon told Alison affably, as he climbed down from the stool. 'We're going to open a large tin of salmon, so there will be plenty for everyone. Do you like salmon?'

'Yes, I do, very much,' Alison told him.

'When he says salmon he means the tinned stuff,' David told her. 'He simply loves it, while he hates the real thing. It seems a strange preference here in the Highlands, but that's the way it is with Simon. If you like the tinned variety too you've forged a bond which may well last for life.'

'Oh, Simon and I got on very well, right from the moment we first met,' Alison smiled at the boy as he ran out to play with Correy in the garden.

'Yes, so I've noticed,' David said thoughtfully and with a certain significance so that Alison hurriedly asked, 'Now where do you keep the tablecloths?'

'I'm dashed if I know,' David told her. 'I hadn't thought of troubling about the niceties this evening. However, if you feel that we should—'

Eventually Alison found the tablecloths neatly stacked in a tall oak cupboard in the narrow passage leading out of the kitchen. But there were none of the bright red or blue and white checked tablecloths which would have been suitable for a kitchen tea and reluctantly she picked out a cloth of snowy linen with a lace edging. Upon this they placed the old rose-patterned china and a honey jar shaped like a beehive. David eventually made use of his bread-saw by slicing up a large crusty loaf on a round wooden board adorned with the words 'Bread is the staff of life' and embellished around the edge with carved ears of wheat.

'Now, let me see, what else should there be?' David was murmuring as he surveyed the table. 'Somehow it looks very bare to me. Oh yes, I remember now, we have a tin of bannocks somewhere.'

With Alison's assistance, he discovered not only a tin of bannocks, which the provident housekeeper had baked before her departure, but also a napkin of wheaten scones and a great wedge of black bun. The lid of the big black iron kettle was jingling musically on the anthracite stove by the time Alison had grilled the streaky rashers Lowrie preferred to salmon. Simon, who had run into the house again, was munching a piece of black bun which Alison had secretly sliced off and slipped to him when at last Lowrie and Hester returned from their lesson.

As Hester's eyes fell upon Alison it was clear that her presence was anything but welcome.

'We can have tea now the lesson is over, can't we?' Simon demanded, picking up the big brown earthenware tea-pot. 'I'll make the tea. I know how. One spoon each and one for the pot.'

'Give that to me.' David took the tea-pot firmly from his son's hand before he could dash it upon the ground in his excitement.

Alison made tea, while Hester engaged David in conversation. She was dressed in a bright scarlet trouser suit and was wearing very high-heeled open shoes which were decidedly muddy from her walk along the river path.

'May I bring Correy into the house?' Simon asked.

But already he had done so, and Alison was dismayed to see the little dog jumping up on Hester and trying to lick her hand.

'Do get down,' Hester said impatiently, pushing him away. 'Now just look at what he's done to my clothes!' And there, plainly visible against the bright, glowing scarlet of her suit, was the print of his muddy paws.

'Don't know what I'd have done without Alison.' David flashed Alison a grateful glance. 'She's saved our lives this evening. There would have been no tea ready for your return if she hadn't turned to, and worked like a slave.'

'Oh yes, Alison's wonderful,' Hester said sourly. 'Everyone says so. As for me, I'm completely undomesticated. So you may as well know that right away.'

There was a silence after this, although Alison was aware that David was amused by Hester's remark. Then they sat down to tea. Lowrie murmured a grace and they began to eat.

'Have some black bun,' Simon piped after a little while.

'No, thanks,' Hester replied with emphasis. 'I simply hate black bun.'

'And you hate tinned salmon too,' Simon told her. 'You hate everything I like, and that means that we won't be lifelong friends because there's no bond between us.'

'Take your tea,' David broke in quickly.

173

'And Hester, tell me, how are you getting along with the lessons?'

'Oh, very well,' Hester assured him. 'I'm learning a new tune now—Handel's Largo.'

'Oh, so that's what it was,' David murmured, pretending to choke on a crumb; he coughed and had to be patted on the back by his son, who climbed up on his chair to perform this act of ministry.

'I've really no ear for music,' David told her when he had recovered somewhat. 'I thought the tune was familiar, but couldn't place it.'

'You're rotten at the organ,' Simon told Hester candidly. 'I've to put my hands over my ears when you play, you're so bad.'

'That will do, Simon!' Lowrie said repressively.

'Really, David,' Hester had flushed angrily, 'have you no control over the child? He's extraordinarily impudent. Anyway, it's a lie. Lowrie here told me I'm coming along nicely.'

'It's not a lie! It's not a lie!' piped Simon indignantly. 'He said that because you're only a girl and would cry like anything if he told you the truth. But he told Daddy you're the worst pupil he ever had.'

'Hush!' cried Lowrie, embarrassed. 'Be silent, Simon!'

'This is really too much!' cried Hester, springing to her feet. 'I've stood enough from

174

that child, David. Make him apologise at once!'

'I won't apologise!' bawled Simon. 'It's the truth, isn't it, Daddy?'

Faced with this situation, David attempted to temporise. 'Oh, do sit down, Hester,' he told her with an attempt at good-humoured bonhomie. 'You're making far too much of a bit of childish nonsense.'

But Hester was not to be put off. 'I'm warning you, David. Either he apologises or I leave the house this minute!' she announced.

It was only too plain that Simon had been recounting the truth when once again David attempted to put her off. 'Oh, do be sensible, Hester. All little boys are rude—outspoken and—'

'Apologise, Simon!' Hester turned in fury to the child.

'I won't: it's the truth!' cried Simon, frightened and defiant, and bursting into a storm of sobs he ran from the room.

'You realize that you've deliberately refused to make him apologise,' Hester turned in a cold fury to David. 'I'm not going to take any more of this!' and picking up her music she swept out of the cottage. They could hear the thud as she slammed the outer door and the sound of her footsteps ringing on the short garden path as she walked away.

In the silence that followed her departure, Lowrie said in his soft voice, 'You know,

175

David, Hester's right: Simon is getting completely out of hand. He's running wild about the countryside, coming home with his clothes torn and his legs and arms scratched. Only the other day he tumbled into the burn and came in soaking and chilled to the bone.'

'And what am I to do about it?' David demanded, exasperated. 'I can't watch a child of that age every moment of the day. Anyway, I'll have to be getting back to work soon. This Highland holiday can't go on for ever.'

'I don't expect you to watch Simon yourself,' Lowrie replied with dignity. 'What I'm trying to convey to you is that he should have a woman's care. He wouldn't be half so wild and unmanageable if he had a woman's love now when he's at the age when he needs it.' As he spoke his eyes were on Alison.

In the silence that followed Alison was aware that although David did not glance at her, he was acutely conscious of her presence. She glanced at her watch. 'Really, I must be going,' she muttered, getting to her feet.

'You must take Alison home,' Lowrie told David. 'It's growing dusk already.'

'I fully intended to do that,' David told his great-uncle, a little resentfully.

'I'll take care of Simon and see that he gets off to bed at a reasonable time,' Lowrie told them as he saw them off at the door.

In silence David and Alison began to walk

back along the riverside path, Correy weaving circles around them as they went along. 'Really, sometimes Lowrie annoys me,' David said at last. 'He's always saying how out of hand Simon has become, yet what am I to do about it? I can't stay here in Abercorrey for ever. It's time I got back to work again. Lowrie's right,' he finished ruefully, 'I am in a bit of a pickle, yet I can't take up my life again until I've done something about Simon. I could leave him here with my great-uncle, but it wouldn't really be any solution to my problem.'

They walked in through the gates of Abercorrey and as they went along the drive, dimly through the twilight, they could see the low shape of the cottage. 'It was there you grew up, wasn't it?' David asked, stopping to survey it.

As Alison followed his glance she thought how desolate the cottage now looked surrounded by trees and against the dark background of the great overgrown holly hedge. 'Yes, at one time I loved it,' she told him. 'But now I'm glad I'm not living there. When I invited myself to Abercorrey I thought I should be staying here, because Seaton always said I might regard it as my very own, but to tell the truth I'm rather relieved it has fallen into disrepair and that he has given me a room at the main house.'

As they were speaking they had strolled

along the narrow winding path which led towards the cottage and as it came more clearly into view, David said, 'Yes, it does look desolate. You would have been very lonely staying here by yourself, Alison. As lonely as I am,' he added in a softer voice. 'But then I've been lonely for a long time—long before Sylvia was killed. I'm giving you my confidence, Alison, when I tell you that Sylvia didn't care for me—not during the last few years of our marriage.'

Alison was silent. How could she tell him that this was not news to her, that Keith had revealed that Sylvia Inglis had been bored by her husband and had sought adventures outside their marriage?

'In fact, our marriage was already quite broken up at the time Sylvia was killed,' David went on abruptly, 'so that you needn't think me heartlessly prompt to take a wife if I ask you now, Alison, if you could care for me.'

'David—' she tried to stop him.

They had moved forward until they stood shadowed by the great wild holly hedge. He could not see her expression and hurried on. 'I won't pretend that I'm a romantic fellow—not any longer. I think Sylvia's unfaithfulness killed something in me that will never live again. But with all my faults I think I would make a fairly good if unromantic husband to any woman who would risk marrying me. There is also the problem of Simon. Without flattering myself I believe that there would have been women who would have cared for me but who couldn't face the idea of being saddled with an unruly stepson. However, you seem to like him and to get along with him well, so perhaps that wouldn't be as great a problem in your case as it would be in others. What do you say, do you think we could make a go of things?'

They were standing on the very spot where Keith used to come and throw pebbles up at her window on those evenings so long ago and now Alison reached up and plucked a leaf from the holly hedge. As she turned it in her fingers in the twilight she felt rather than saw the shining darkness of the green surface, the curving tip and the short sharp thorns along the edge of the leaf. She would not marry David, she knew instantly, but how to word her refusal so as to hurt his feelings as little as possible!

'It's true, David,' she began, 'that I like Simon and I do believe that we would get along. Apart from that I—'

'Then you're accepting me!' As he spoke he put his arms around her and began to kiss her passionately. 'Oh, Alison, this is wonderful! More wonderful than I dared to hope.'

'No, David,' she struggled out of his arms. 'You're mistaken. I was going to say that I like you tremendously but that I could never, never marry you.'

As she spoke there was a loud rustling sound behind the hedge and a figure darted out and rushed off in the direction of the house.

'What was that?' Alison cried, turning too late to see more than a dim fleeing figure.

'That was Hester,' he told her dryly. 'She must have crept up and hid behind the hedge.'

Hester had lingered about the gates of Abercorrey waiting for her return, Alison guessed. She had surmised that David would accompany her home in the twilight and consumed by jealousy she had resolved to eavesdrop on their conversation. She could hardly have anticipated that what she would hear would be David's proposal.

But whatever Hester had intended, she had effectually broken up their tête-à-tête. Alison continued towards the house with Correy and, when she had made sure he was safe in the straw-filled pen in the stable which was his bed for the night, she went indoors completely unprepared for the scene which met her in the hall. Geralda reclined sprawled in an armchair while Keith was striding up and down, a furious expression on his face.

He swung around as she entered. 'Congratulations on your engagement,' he said tightly.

'What do you mean?' Alison asked.

'I mean your engagement to David, of course,' Keith told her. 'You don't deny it, I suppose.'

Her first impulse was to tell him the truth, but annoyed at his angry manner, she said as coolly as she could, 'So Hester has been telling tales, as usual.'

As she spoke she moved across the hall, picked up a magazine and seated herself, turning the pages with as great a show of nonchalance as she could. What could Hester have meant by spinning such a yarn? Alison wondered—not that there was much sense in any of Hester's lies. 'Where is Hester anyway?' she asked.

'Poor little Hester has retired to her room in a flood of tears.' Geralda sounded bored. 'It seems she'll never, never forgive you for stealing the only man she could ever love. Although, come to think of it, her parting words were that she intended to tackle David in the morning and beg him to reconsider—for his own good, you understand. Really, one pities David. Does she think he's going to remain a widower until she grows up?'

'When you've quite finished discussing Hester, perhaps we could return to the subject of Alison's engagement,' Keith said with such savage intensity that Geralda replied with annoyance. 'By all means, but surely Alison is old enough to decide for herself. One can carry paternalism *too* far, you know.'

'Would it be paternalism if I were to ask one simple, straightforward question? Are you or are you not engaged to David?' he demanded of Alison.

But by now Alison was stubbornly determined not to reply. 'You should ask Hester that. She seems to know my business much better than I do myself. But then why shouldn't she, when she was hidden behind the holly hedge eavesdropping on us?'

'So that's where it took place!' exclaimed Keith. 'By the holly hedge near the cottage.'

'I've seen that place,' Geralda said musingly. 'And really it's ideal for the purpose—so dark and romantic! No girl could bring herself to refuse a man who proposed in such a suitable spot.'

'But David! Don't tell me you're in love with him!' Keith challenged Alison.

'What business is it of yours,' she snapped, 'whether I'm in love with him or not?'

'Hester seems to think you are,' Geralda said thoughtfully. 'She said you were "kissing like anything". She seems to have felt you should have sealed the bargain with a warm handshake. And really, Keith, all this harping about whether she's in love with David or not! The fact remains that they were kissing. You don't deny that, do you, my dear?' she challenged Alison. 'And why on earth should you? There's no crime in a little bit of smooching.'

Then, as Alison remained silent, she went on smoothly, 'What else a girl is to do here in the heart of the country except kiss behind holly hedges, I really don't know. Whether she is or is not in love is completely immaterial.'

'I've had enough of this,' cried Alison, springing to her feet. 'I'm not going to listen to another word!' As she spoke, she threw down the magazine and ran upstairs.

To her surprise she became aware of Keith's footsteps springing up the stairs behind her. He made up with her as she drew near to the door of her room, caught her by the elbow and swung her around to face him. 'Is it true?' he demanded.

Again, for an instant she was about to deny it, but his fierce face pushed close to her antagonised her. 'What if I am engaged?' she retorted. 'It's none of your business.'

'Perhaps not,' he gritted. 'But then of course the past means nothing to you. You've thrown it overboard like trash. You're starting a new life with David now, who's smooth and charming and knows how to be popular in any society; while I'm ugly and scarred, and uncouth and unpopular. But to have chosen the spot by the holly hedge for your engagement scene! The place that was ours; where we used to meet so often. You've a short memory, Alison!'

Alison drew in her breath in indignation. To think that he dared speak to her in this strain while he was openly pursuing Geralda and had completely ignored her since her arrival! 'It wasn't I who forgot: it was you!' she flashed.

As she spoke she pulled her arm abruptly from his grasp, swung around, entered her room and slammed the door angrily behind her, leaving him standing in the corridor.

CHAPTER NINE

On the following morning Alison was standing near one of the windows of her room, drawing the brush through her short dark hair. The vista of moorland and mountain was wonderful, but perhaps the most striking thing was the view of the Correy at the spot where the giant boulder stood in the middle of the river. At this time of the year, when winter was almost upon the Highlands, the rushing waters were flung upwards in a great spray.

She paused, brush in hand, as there was a tap on the door and to her surprise Geralda entered.

Alison, standing at the window, was partly

hidden by the long damask drapes. She saw Geralda look about the room and towards the bed, as though half expecting that she might not yet be up. Then, seeing that the room was apparently empty, she was just about to go out again when Alison called, 'I'm here by the window.'

'Oh, there you are.' Geralda crossed the room to join her.

There was a short silence and Alison looked at her inquiringly, but to her surprise Geralda seemed to have some difficulty in beginning. Obviously to give herself time to make a start, she turned to the window and following Alison's gaze, said, 'Whew, what a terrific view! If you like that type of thing. This used to be the first Mrs Heseltine's room, I believe.'

'Yes, that's so,' Alison told her. 'I was just looking at the boulder in the middle of the river and remembering how Ian used to dive from it into the river.'

'I've heard a lot about this Ian since I've come,' Geralda said curiously. 'Everyone here seems to have worshipped him. He must have been a very extraordinary sort of person.'

'Yes, Ian was wonderful in many ways. He was very handsome and very athletic and was one of the best divers, although he was not as strong a swimmer as Keith.'

'You sound all in admiration of him,' Geralda said a little sourly. 'It's a wonder you

185

didn't fall for him if he was so attractive.'

'Oh, I admired Ian,' Alison said consideringly. 'You couldn't help doing that. He had amazing charm and could captivate almost everyone he came across—and yet there was something about him that I could never like: he struck me as being a selfish and self-centred person.'

'In other words, you gave your heart to Keith!'

'Oh, that's all in the past—a boy-and-girl affair,' Alison said quietly. 'It doesn't mean anything now.'

'Oh, doesen't it!' Geralda retorted. 'Perhaps it's all in the past as far as you're concerned, but when it comes to Keith it's a different matter! Last evening, when we heard you'd become engaged to David, he was furious—whether it was wounded vanity or not, I don't know, but it puts me in a horrible position. He's keen on me, I know, but never in my life before have I had to play second fiddle to what are nothing more than a man's nostalgic memories—for that's really all that lies between you. In a million ways he's shown you that marriage isn't in his mind, as far as you're concerned. However, now that you've accepted David's proposal things will straighten out.'

'In what way?' Alison asked, a little puzzled.

'Well, for one thing, David must take up

his life again, which will probably mean you'll be moving back to the south of England with him. That will leave the coast clear for me, for up till now you've been playing dog-in-the-manger, constantly reminding Keith of that boy-and-girl affair. It's not fair to me. Now that you're engaged to David you should show Keith clearly that the past is over. I never had to beg and plead with another woman before, but now I'm doing it. Clear out and give me a chance with Keith, because as far as I'm concerned this is the real thing. I never in my life felt about any man as I do about him. I've really fallen for him. He's the only man in the world for me and—'

Just then, to Alison's relief, there was a tap on the door and one of the young maids brought the message that there was a phone call for Alison. There was no phone extension in Flora's room and Alison decided to take the call in the hall. It would be deserted at this time and it would give her the excuse of getting away from Geralda's embarrassing onslaught.

Her mind was still buzzing with her extraordinary interview with Geralda as she crossed the wide hall and picked up the receiver which was in a nook near the great main door. The call would be from David, she surmised, or perhaps from the village dressmaker, who was making an alteration to one of her dresses.

She was amazed to hear the deep, pompous tones of Toby Benson.

'Hello, Alison, I'm sure you're surprised to hear from me—and stranger still, I'm speaking from Aberdeen. This is Toby speaking.'

But of course she had recognised his tones immediately! From the corner of her eye she had also seen Keith enter the hall, stroll across to the wide chimney-piece and stand with his back to the fire which always burned there, summer and winter.

'Toby!' Alison's exclamation was louder than she intended. 'In Aberdeen! What on earth are you doing there?'

'Don't tell me that's the Toby Benson who threw you over for Geralda?'

And Alison swung around to find that Keith had crossed the hall and was standing close beside her.

'Go away!' she hissed, but he paid no attention, remaining in a listening posture, his head cocked attentively.

'Well, you might say I'm in Aberdeen on business,' Toby told her. 'But really, to be perfectly honest, it was with the hope that I could see you and that we could have a chat. Could you possibly meet me?'

'Meet you? In Aberdeen?' repeated Alison. 'But I couldn't possibly. I'm—I'm busy.'

'What do you mean "busy"?' Keith's mouth was close to her ear, his voice low and teasing. 'You know that's a direct falsehood, Alison Lennox! Why don't you meet the poor fellow? I'm perfectly sure he's going to apologise for throwing you over for Geralda.'

His guess was borne out by Toby saying on the line, 'You know, Alison, I can't say how sorry I am that things turned out as they did between us. At least give me the opportunity to say how sorry I am.'

'There's no need for an apology,' Alison told him. 'I quite understand.'

'Oh, do let him apologise,' Keith's voice hissed in her ear. 'It will do him good to get it off his chest. Go on, I dare you. I'll bet you're too cowardy custard to meet him.'

'Oh, do shut up!' Alison said desperately, holding her hand over the receiver.

But she hesitated about giving Toby a direct refusal. Suddenly there came into her mind Geralda's remarks about her being dog-in-the-manger as far as Keith was concerned. Geralda had been right in saying that Keith now no longer cared for her. 'In a million ways he has shown you that marriage isn't in his mind as far as you're concerned.' It was these words of Geralda's that made her eventually agree to meet Toby.

She was conscious of the relieved and pleased tone in Toby's voice as he made an appointment for lunch at one of Aberdeen's leading hotels.

'Very well, see you at lunch, then.

Goodbye, Toby,' she said.

'Lunch, where?' came Keith's inquisitive question.

Before she had time to stop herself she had told him and then she rounded on him angrily. 'How dare you listen in to my telephone conversation,' she blazed, 'and butt in, in that rude fashion, every few minutes! You're a bad-mannered, insufferable boor, and—'

'I've never pretended to possess gentlemanly instincts, have I?' he asked with an air of reasonableness.

'No, you certainly haven't,' she answered furiously.

'David should watch out for himself,' Keith told her, a gleam in his eye. 'He doesn't know what a savage, bad-tempered, primitive bundle of female ferocity he's tying himself to for life. I pity the poor fellow: he obviously has no idea of what he's letting himself in for.'

Alison turned away without replying and marched across the hall in the direction of the stairs. But he followed her.

'By the way,' he began, his hand on the great carved newel post, 'there seems to be some ambiguity about whether you are or are not engaged to David. You gave no clear answer yesterday evening to our enquiries. Naturally we're interested.'

'It's no business of yours!' she flashed.

190

'I see,' he said thoughtfully. 'So perhaps we're to take it that there's still a chance for poor old Toby?'

'Now what do you mean by that remark?' Alison asked exasperatedly.

'I mean of course that Toby has come not only to apologise but to propose once more. What else could have made him brave the journey from the south of England to the wilds of Scotland?'

'He's here on a business trip and just rang me up to say hello,' Alison told him, 'and I heartily wish I hadn't let you dare me into meeting him.'

'A business trip indeed!' scoffed Keith. 'An obvious lie! Why, Hester could do better than that! It's the sort of transparent fabrication that men make up to give themselves some defensive covering when they're crazy about a girl and can't live without her.'

'Toby seems to have been able to live without me—for a long time, too,' Alison told him dryly.

'But he's back under your spell now,' he told her. 'You know, Alison, once you were a long-legged girl with scratched knees and tousled hair, but from all appearances I must admit that time has apparently transformed you into a breaker of hearts. First there's David hanging on your words and ignoring the beautiful Geralda, and now this Toby panting to apologise abjectly and to lay his heart at your feet once more. There's no doubt about it the scruffy, bad-tempered, grubby girl I once knew has developed into a *femme fatale*.'

He was mocking her, she knew. As she gazed at him Alison was thinking that David did perhaps care for her, but merely as a mother for Simon. He had made no secret of the fact that he was disillusioned as far as marriage was concerned. Perhaps Toby had, in fact, come to Aberdeen to propose. But as for her being a breaker of hearts—the one heart she would have wished to touch—Keith's—was given to Geralda.

'And another thing—I was never grubby,' she informed him with dignity as she began to mount the stairs.

'Yes, you were, often,' he called after her, 'though no doubt now that you've turned into a *femme fatale* you'd prefer to forget your disreputable past.'

She turned half-way up the stairs. 'Oh, you're despicable!' she informed him, exasperatedly.

He flung back his head and burst into laughter. 'That's my old Alison speaking,' and continued before turning away, 'Not the dignified young lady with proposals fluttering at her feet.'

In her own room once more Alison made up carefully for her lunch date with Toby. He liked her to appear at her best when she went out with him, she knew, and she changed into one of her prettiest frocks and put on clip ear-rings and a long chunky necklace which hung below her waist.

But as she drove into Aberdeen her thoughts were not on Toby but on her conversation with Geralda earlier that morning. She was inclined to think that Geralda's analysis of Keith's attitude towards her was correct. He still cared for her—cared enough to worry if she were out too late. But his concern stemmed from their relationship of the past. It was something protective and not the adult love that she now desired from him.

Which brought her to the problem of Toby. He had, she knew, many good qualities: he was kind and conscientious and industrious; he would make a good husband—and doubtless a faithful one now that Geralda's influence had been removed from his life. As to Keith, she would do well to put him out of her mind, now that Geralda had come upon the scene.

Keith was the second man Geralda had taken from her, Alison was thinking as she drove slowly along King Street and parked the car in the garage used by the Heseltines. And no doubt if she hadn't fallen for him so completely she would have amused herself and relieved her boredom with the Highlands in exerting all her charm on David. But in

Keith Geralda had at last met a man who was her match and typically enough had decided he was the only one for her.

As she entered the foyer of the hotel, Toby got up out of the deep lounging chairs. He had grown stouter. Suddenly it seemed to her that he looked soft and plump with a curious air of premature middle-age. Perhaps it was that he exuded an air of affluence accentuated by the clothes he wore. He too, had dressed carefully for the occasion, she knew, noting his perfectly tailored expensive suit and quiet dark-toned tie. And as soon as she saw his expectant expression she knew that Keith had been right when he said that Toby intended to propose once more.

They went in to the table he had reserved in one of the restaurants and here Toby ordered an expensive, well-chosen meal and paid her the ponderous compliments that were his idea of suitable conversation at the beginning of a meal. When he told her how beautiful she looked Alison discounted the word 'beautiful', but she knew that her appearance had improved since her arrival at Correybrae. A little colour had come into her cheeks, she was less thin and had shed the worn look she had had in those days when the full care of the boutique had been upon her shoulders. Now, instead of snatching a sandwich and a cup of coffee at odd moments, she ate well, slept soundly and went for long walks through the moors with Correy.

From the necessary compliments Toby moved on to talk about Market Hanboury and the people they had both known there. She found that she was enjoying the snippets of gossip he was retailing about mutual acquaintances there when she looked up and saw that directly across the room from her, at a table for two, sat Keith and Geralda. They appeared to be engrossed in each other. For a moment Alison wondered if their presence was mere coincidence. After all, this was one of Aberdeen's most expensive restaurants. This was very probably where Keith and Geralda were accustomed to lunch during those long days they spent together. On the other hand it would be typical of Keith to deliberately select the hotel in which he knew she was meeting Toby. No doubt, with typical effrontery, he hoped that his presence would prove embarrassing to her.

As the meal drew to a close Toby became more serious. 'I suppose you know why I'm here, Alison,' he began, rather shamefacedly. 'I want you to know what a fool I made of myself. Now when I look back upon it I can hardly believe I was crazy enough to take up with Geralda. She's completely shallow and superficial, I should have realized more and more that you were the only girl for me. I asked you to meet me today so that I could tell you that I freely admit I made a dreadful mistake and to ask you if you could possibly bring yourself to forgive me and—'

'Why, Toby Benson, and what are you doing in Aberdeen?' Alison glanced up and found Geralda beside them. Her eyes slid from Toby to Alison.

Toby looked up, his colour heightening as he caught sight of her. 'Geralda!' It was obvious that this meeting with her again was highly embarrassing and unwelcome to him.

Geralda, however, was perfectly at ease. As Keith joined them she said with cool self-possession, 'You two haven't met, have you?'

'But you haven't told us what you're doing so far away from home,' Geralda returned to the attack when she had introduced the two men.

'Oh, just a business trip,' Toby muttered. 'I happened to be here and—'

'Well, if this is your first visit to the north you mustn't let it be said that we Hielanders are inhospitable,' Keith broke in with a geniality that Alison was fully aware was assumed. 'If you're doing nothing better this evening I insist you join us for dinner.'

'Thanks, but—' Toby began.

'Have you a car here?' Keith inquired, and when Toby told him that he had arranged a self-drive hire, Keith burst in with overwhelming hospitality, 'Now don't give a thought to a car. If you've nothing better to do this afternoon why not drive back with us now and we would have the pleasure of your company for the rest of the afternoon.'

'Thanks, but—' Toby began again. 'You see, Alison and I haven't met for some time. We've quite a lot to talk about, and—'

'But you can chat away to your hearts' content about old times in the car as we return to Abercorrey,' Keith insisted. 'Don't you think it's a good idea, Alison?' His dark eyes appeared to question her, but there was no concealing the glint of mockery in them.

Alison was aware of Toby's gaze fixed on her face and she reluctantly agreed; knowing the plodding stubbornness of his character, she felt sure that he would never give up until he had proposed and either been accepted or rejected.

Of one thing she was perfectly certain as they got into the car and drove back together to Abercorrey, and that was that Keith was up to mischief. And whatever chance they might have had of having a quiet conversation during the drive was quite spoiled by Keith's pointing out places of historical interest and insisting on playing the solicitous host for the entire journey.

When they arrived at Abercorrey he contrived to fill in the afternoon by insisting on carrying off Toby to look at the stables and other parts of the estate, keeping up a steady spate of small talk so that Toby was unable to snatch a quiet moment alone with Alison.

At dinner that evening Alison was aware that everyone had gone to pains to look their best. Geralda came down in one of her loveliest dresses of lime green chiffon, she herself had taken trouble to look her best and Morag was wearing what she evidently considered a festive number of green and red tartan. A newcomer was rather an event for Morag, who was very much tied to the house because of Seaton's semi-invalid way of life. But she was looking particularly content because Seaton had come down to dinner in honour of the guest and was exerting himself to play the gracious host as he always did with strangers.

Toby, looking a little confused and bewildered after his session with Keith, attempted to make conversation. 'Don't you miss the boutique, Alison? Or do the beauties of the Highlands compensate completely? At one time it was your whole life, I know.'

'Oh, Alison has new interests here,' Geralda said with lazy contempt. 'She has a perfectly wonderful sheepdog, a marvel of intelligence which she's training so that it may win the prizes at the sheepdog trials.'

Toby glanced questioningly at Alison for a moment, then laughed dutifully. It was clear that he did not know how to take this remark. 'Doesn't sound so fascinating after the excitement of the world of fashion. What must it have been to fly to Paris or Rome on buying trips! However satisfied Alison is with life in the country it must be a great blow to you, Geralda, to see how the boutique has slipped since Alison withdrew from the scene.'

Alison glanced at him. Was this a typical bit of tactlessness on his part or was it a malicious dig at her whom he doubtless must now dislike intensely after the way she had picked him up and then casually dropped?

'I know the boutique has fallen off since Alison "withdrew from the scene" as you put it, Toby,' Geralda snapped. 'And I've tried to get her back again, promised her any salary she wishes if she'll return, but she's not interested—so she must prefer the mists of the Highlands to the delights of Market Hanboury.'

There was a short silence after this outburst and Keith said with a great assumption of interest, 'So that's why you were motoring through the Highlands and just happened to drop in on Alison at Abercorrey. You came to beg Alison to return on her own terms, is that it?'

As Geralda remained silent, Morag looked slightly aggrieved. 'And you told us you were going around the Highlands looking at and ordering hand-knitted garments. I was so pleased, for we really have some wonderful things—so much nicer than those weird, surrealist-designed garments one sees in all the shops.'

Geralda had the grace to look embarrassed. 'No, not altogether true,' she said. 'I came to ask Alison to come back. But those "weird surrealist garments", as you term them, were exactly what sold so well in my boutique,' she added tight-lipped. Hester, who was listening eagerly, glanced across at Alison with new respect. 'How I envy you: I'd just love that sort of life.'

Seaton, who had been sitting silent, eyed his daughter quizzically. 'You mean you'd actually desert David for a more glamorous type of life?'

Hester's cheeks grew pink. She toyed with her fork, looking suddenly very youthful in spite of her upswept hair and dangling ear-rings. 'Oh, I don't mean that, but if I hadn't met David it's the kind of life I'd love: travelling about and meeting all sorts of interesting people and buying heaps of gorgeous clothes. I can't imagine why Alison could have given it up to come here. It must be so deadly dull after leading the sort of life she's used to.'

Alison was aware of Seaton's eyes resting on her questioningly.

'Oh no, you're quite wrong, Hester. I simply love it here,' Alison said hastily.

'But of course she does,' Geralda

announced coolly. 'The boutique must have very little to offer Alison compared to the superior attractions of Abercorrey. If I'd known how she felt about things I wouldn't have wasted my breath asking her to come back to Hanboury in the first place.'

Toby, puzzled by the ambiguity of the remark, turned to Alison. 'But I understood you loved working at the boutique. I mean, Abercorrey is all right for a holiday, but—' He stopped, growing a dusky red as he realized where his tactlessness was leading him.

'But that's just where you're wrong, Toby,' Geralda put in. 'Hasn't it occurred to you that far from considering Abercorrey as a holiday, Alison was planning to make it a fixture?'

For a moment there was silence and Alison was aware that she was the focus of all eyes—Toby's puzzled and uneasy, Keith's dancing with mockery at her dilemma.

It was Seaton who, with typical courtesy, retrieved the situation. 'When Alison first came here I had the hope she might consider Abercorrey as her permanent home, but the decision, of course, was up to her.'

It was at this point that, much to Alison's relief, Morag with one of her typically gauche movements upset her glass and the incident was sufficient to put an end to the subject.

But not before Toby announced ponderously, 'I'd certainly hate to see her settle into a way of life that would offer her so little scope for her talents.'

His manner had a curious air of possessiveness and left Alison in no doubt as to what he expected her answer to be when he at last got the opportunity of proposing.

Keith regarded him with an air of mock inquiry. 'You sound extremely solicitous for Alison's welfare. It does you credit.'

Toby smiled complacently. 'Let's say Alison and I have been extremely good friends. I consider her a pretty wonderful person.'

Alison felt herself flush and wished fervently that Toby would call a halt to his embarrassing eulogy.

Morag, however, seemed delighted at the fulsome compliment and she regarded Toby approvingly. 'Yes indeed, we all value Alison very much and consider ourselves lucky to have her with us. After dinner you must show your guest the rose garden. Most of the roses have gone by now, of course,' she added to Toby, 'but a few remain in sheltered spots. But put a wrap on,' she added to Alison. 'The evening is mild for this time of the year, but still there's a sting in the air.'

When eventually they left the dining-room, Alison hesitated a moment, debating with herself Morag's advice. The thought of the proposal ahead did not attract her. At the same time, knowing Toby, she had no hopes that he would take his departure until everything had been thrashed out.

She went up to her room and fetched a silk scarf that had been one of her buys for the boutique. It was wonderfully becoming, the soft folds surrounding her small, piquant face and the silky fringe floating over her shoulders and down her back.

Morag waylaid her as she came downstairs again. 'I hope you didn't mind my butting in,' she apologised with her usual diffident manner, 'but I could see that this Toby of yours is very much in love with you. He seems to be a fine person and I'm sure he would make a good husband. If you like him you should encourage him. I'd like to see you married to a man who cared for you and who would try to make you happy.' She hesitated, then gave Alison a quick embrace before hurrying downstairs.

'Now where is this last rose of summer our hostess was so anxious I should see?' Toby asked, a little sardonically, when she joined him in the garden.

Alison laughed. 'I'm afraid Morag's a bit obvious. But she's a fine person and I think she likes you.'

'Well, pleased as I am that she approves of me,' Toby told her, 'I'd be even more delighted if I knew that you liked me too. As I was trying to tell you this afternoon at lunch when we were interrupted, I've made a fool of myself, I admit it, but I ask you to forgive me. If you could look upon me as a person with whom you could spend the remainder of—'

It was here that Keith appeared from a side path. He was holding a dried twig upon which hung pathetically a shrivelled rose. 'To think that this was once a glorious Violet Carson,' he said. 'But I'm afraid the frost has got at it.'

'How interesting,' Toby replied with a frostiness to match the autumn evening.

But Keith seemed impervious to Toby's annoyance. 'Now over here we had a splendid McGredy's Yellow and this was Peace—Chicago Peace, I'm sorry to say. You don't mind my showing you around,' his voice sounded apologetic, 'but I could see right away as soon as Morag suggested your seeing the garden that you were a rose fancier and I was so afraid you'd be bored. You see, Alison, clever as she is, is not knowledgeable about roses. She hardly knows a floribunda from a hybrid tea. Now over here we have—'

As Keith led them around the rose garden pointing out the shrivelled bushes which had once held great masses of fragrant blooms, Alison could feel Toby grow more and more impatient. So Keith was determined to keep up his harassing tactics, she thought angrily. After all, Toby was her guest and this baiting and embarrassing of him was insupportable, so after a few minutes she brought it firmly to a halt by saying. 'If you don't mind, Keith, I wonder if you'd leave us.'

'Oh, am I butting in?' Keith asked with simulated surprise, so that Alison found herself gritting her teeth with annoyance. 'Why, I wouldn't have done that for the world!' And off he went with every mockery of being subdued and embarrassed by his own tactlessness.

When eventually his footsteps died away on the flagged walk Toby tried once more to propose, but Keith had succeeded in destroying the romantic mood and after one or two incoherent attempts to begin again he gave up, and eventually they walked back to the house in an embarrassed silence.

Seated near the great chimneypiece in the hall they found Keith and Geralda. Of Hester there was no sign and Alison supposed that Seaton had also retired: he would have gone to his room, fatigued by the effort of putting in an appearance for the sake of their guest.

Keith raised his thick black eyebrows. 'Well, well, have you exhausted the pleasures of the rose garden so soon?'

'Not quite,' Toby said sourly, 'but it was getting too cold.'

'Yes, it is late in the year for dallying in gardens, however important the subject of conversation.' His keen glance moved from Toby's disgruntled face to Alison's on which annoyance was plainly written.

Whatever he read in their expressions seemed to afford him extreme satisfaction. 'Geralda and I have been discussing the Correybrae Gathering, which takes place tomorrow. You're looking forward to this event keenly, aren't you?' he asked Geralda with a gleam in his eye.

'It promises to be the highlight of my visit to the Highlands,' Geralda returned with elaborate irony. 'What with prizes for the best madeira cake—'

'Not to mention the cut-throat competition for the best knitted socks,' Keith put in.

'There's to be a prize for home-made wine this year, I believe,' Geralda went on. 'That should be simply fascinating. Oh, Keith, surely we could get out of it. *Must* we attend?'

'I'm afraid we must,' he told her. 'Our absence would be noted. But the home-made goodies aren't all that's to it. I'm sure if you live in the south of England you've never seen the tossing of the caber,' he said to Toby. 'What do you say you stay on and take a look at it? It may be years before you're in the Highlands again—if ever—' he added, glancing at Alison. 'And it would be a pity to miss the opportunity of seeing something of the peculiarities of the region.'

Geralda sat up straighter as Keith issued this very unexpected invitation. 'But Toby would be horribly bored,' she protested.

206

'Impossible,' Keith told her. 'No one could fail to be thrilled by the great apple jelly tussle. You see, the dominie's housekeeper, Mrs McPhee, has won first prize for her apple jelly, three years running, but this year our Mrs Fleming has made a truly heroic effort. I've tasted her concoction myself and don't see how it could be beaten. We're waiting with bated breath to see if she'll be able to wrest the prize from the holder tomorrow.'

'Not to mention the sheepdog trials of which we've heard so very much in recent times,' put in Geralda acidly. 'If Alison's dog doesn't win tomorrow we shall all just curl up and die.'

At this piece of news Toby's expression changed. 'So you're interested in this gathering?' he asked Alison. 'You'll be there?'

'Yes, I'll be there,' Alison told him. 'As Geralda has told you, I'm entering a dog in the sheepdog trials and I'm looking forward to seeing how he does.'

'That should be very interesting,' Toby said with a glance at Alison. 'I should certainly like to see it.'

'Then see it you shall,' said Keith warmly.

Toby had made it abundantly clear that now that he knew Alison had an interest in the event, he wished to stay on and accepted the invitation, merely making a token objection that he had no overnight bag, which was quickly overruled by Keith.

'Don't worry about that. We'll be able to give you everything you need.'

He got to his feet with alacrity. 'I'll rustle you up a few things. Come along and we'll get the housekeeper to fix you up.'

When the two men had gone out, Geralda turned to Alison, her face furious. 'Now look at what you've done!' she exclaimed. 'You've brought this embarrassing position on both of us, for I presume you hate it as much as I do. You should at any rate, considering it was Toby who threw you over, whereas it was I who dropped him. What on earth are you playing at, Alison, sneaking off to Aberdeen by yourself today and having lunch with Toby without as much as a word to me although we were talking together just a little while previously. Have you brought Toby here to make David jealous, or something? Although to tell the truth, I don't know what's got into you. Is David not enough for you? One thing is perfectly clear, and that is that Toby is as much in love wih you as he ever was. Don't tell me you're planning to throw David over for him?'

She waited for an answer, her eyes fixed angrily on Alison's face.

And Alison said coldly, 'I resent your tone, Geralda. I'm sick of being spoken to in that way, and I've no intention of discussing my love life with you.' And she stood up and went upstairs without another word.

So for reasons best known to himself Keith had talked Toby into staying on for the Correybrae Gathering, Alison was thinking as she walked along the corridor to her room. How devious he was, this new Keith who had taken the place of the boy she had known. Would she ever be able to understand him?

CHAPTER TEN

There was a flush on the cheeks of the dominie's housekeeper, Mrs McPhee. 'I wouldn't have minded losing fairly,' she was saying, 'but I've tasted your jelly and in all truth I must say that I don't think it measures up to mine.'

'Oh, indeed!' cried Mrs Fleming, bridling.

The two women were in the forefront of a small group who stood in the home produce tent gazing intently at an array of jampots on one of which was stuck a label marked, 'First Prize'.

Towards the back of the crowd Keith caught Alison's eye and winked.

'Well, *I* have tasted *your* jelly, madam,' returned Mrs Fleming, 'and I think the judges were perfectly correct in giving you third prize. In my opinion there was something in the jelling that wasn't quite right. I may say that I use the old-fashioned flannel jelly-bag myself and I think it can't be beaten, although there are some who have taken to they new modern contraptions—but the flavour isn't the same.'

'But surely one doesn't use flannel in making jam,' Toby murmured to Geralda with a touch of alarm.

Geralda raised her shoulders in a shrug of indifference.

'Heaven knows, it's all Greek to me,' she murmured.

'It's the flannel that gives it its peculiar taste,' Keith informed Toby in a low tone. 'Let's clear out before the two ladies come to blows and we're called upon to referee the fight.'

As unobtrusively as possible they detached themselves from the crowd in the tent and went outside—not that their absence was noted by the two ladies, whose voices had risen and whose attention was wholly absorbed in denigrating each other's products.

They had gone only a short distance when their ears were assailed by the bagpipes playing for the competition of strathspeys. On a platform the dancers whirled, their kilts flying. Louder and louder came the music, the pipers' cheeks distended as they blew with might and main, and Geralda clapped her hands over her ears. 'Let's hurry past,' she called, raising her voice to make herself heard. 'What an abominable noise! It would deafen one.'

'You must learn to love the pipes,' Keith told her as they gained a little distance and he was able to make himself heard once more. 'There's no music so thrilling in all the world.'

'Ugh, I hate it,' Geralda told him. 'It sounds to me like a million cats wailing.'

'Don't let Hector hear you say that,' Keith admonished. 'He's a fanatic when it comes to the pipes.'

As they strolled on they saw David, Simon and the dominie approach them. David, after a short greeting, avoided Alison's eye and she too felt rather embarrassed, remembering the circumstances of their last meeting.

Fortunately at that moment Simon hurled himself upon her, holding before him a well licked toffee apple. In his haste his toe caught in a crack in the rough path and in an instant he had tumbled head foremost into her arms, his toffee apple clinging to the front of her suede jacket.

'You may have a lick of the other side, if you wish,' he told her, when they had disentangled themselves. 'It's quite all right: it's perfectly clean. You see I've been licking only on one side and saving the other side until later, but you may have it if you wish.'

David hurried forward. 'Really, Simon, how can you be such a nuisance! I do hope your jacket isn't completely ruined, Alison.'

'Not at all,' Alison smiled. 'The jacket is quite old. I knew better than to turn up in my "good clothes" today.'

They chatted for a moment or two longer, but the ease that had once been in their conversation had quite disappeared and David was obviously glad to return once more to the main group, where he took trouble to attach himself to Toby, Keith and Geralda while Alison fell behind with Lowrie and Simon.

'You may have a bite of my toffee apple,' Simon offered, as though bestowing a great favour, 'because I like you, and—'

'Now, Simon, run off and see if the tea tent is open for customers yet,' Lowrie said firmly.

As Simon ran off eagerly, his toffee apple held out carefully before him, the old man lowered his voice. 'David has been confiding in me that he proposed and that you turned him down. My dear child, I can't say how disappointed I am. Do you not like him? Would you not reconsider?'

'I do like David, immensely,' Alison assured him. 'He's a wonderful person and I only wish I were in love with him. But I'm not, and it wouldn't be fair to him to accept him, feeling as I do.'

'Tell me, Alison my dear, is it because of some fault in David that you are unable to accept him, or is it that you are in love with someone else? You must forgive an old man's curiosity, but I had great hopes that you would accept him and I won't deny that I'm bitterly disappointed.'

She did not reply immediately, but for an instant her eyes went to Keith who was walking in front with Geralda and the old dominie's eyes, following hers, read there the message of that swift unconscious glance. 'I think I know how it is with you, my dear, and although I'm sorry for David's sake, I accept that the heart can't be forced. It has its own logic and knows what it wants. Being in love reminds me of the music of Bach: it has order and serenity in the midst of passion. I know what it is, for I was in love with my dear wife for forty years and we were as much in love after all that time as we were at the beginning. Some love stories are like that—just a very few—and I sincerely hope that you may get your heart's desire.' He sighed. 'But in the meantime things look black for poor David. I know how despondent your refusal has made him.'

Alison wondered if David had confessed to his uncle what he had admitted to her, that disillusionment had made his approach to marriage decidedly unromantic. It was highly unlikely he had done so.

She said cautiously, 'Perhaps it's too early yet for David to think of remarrying: later on

213

he'll probably find a woman to whom he can give his whole heart, and then there will be great happiness ahead for him.'

'You mean that Hester isn't the only girl who will throw herself at his head,' Lowrie smiled. 'Poor child! David's affection for you has been a bitter blow to her, but at least one good thing has come out of it—she has decided to abandon the organ, and to tell the truth I'm heartily relieved, for I don't think that the organ is the instrument for her. Indeed I don't know if Hester is at all musically inclined. Perhaps twanging a guitar is more her line of country. In fact, I think she finds life at Abercorrey dull and uncongenial. At any rate I don't see her here today. No doubt she finds our simple country pleasures tedious.'

'She has gone to Aberdeen with Morag and Seaton,' Alison told him. It might be that Hester's motive in accepting the drive into Aberdeen had been a simple desire to keep out of David's way, but perhaps it might result in a better understanding between her and her stepmother.

But Lowrie wasn't really interested in Hester and very shortly he brought the subject back to David and Alison was relieved when Hector appeared dressed for the momentous occasion in a dark blue suit and bowler hat. For once he had dropped his dour phlegmatic manner. 'Come awa', Miss

Alison,' he called excitedly. 'There's only twa more dogs afore Correy. Ye dinnae want to miss him, do you? You can have a crack with the dominie later on.'

Alison was surprised when they reached the spot from which they could command the area of the trials to find that the other shepherds were, like Hector, dressed in dark suits and bowler hats.

Their group was by now reduced to Toby, Geralda, Keith and Alison, because David had made the excuse that Simon was growing tired to take him off and Lowrie had accompanied them, expressing polite regret that he wouldn't be able to stay to watch Correy's performance.

They watched a couple of dogs in the obedience tests and Alison's heart sank as Number Fifteen went through his paces. This was a big, handsome dog and very alert and obedient, and Alison felt sure he would win.

It was as this dog's trial was coming to an end that Geralda said petulantly, 'I'm simply dying for a cup of tea. The refreshment tent is open and we could slip off.'

At that moment the board went up with 'No. 16' on it, Correy's number, and Keith turned to her with an air of surprise. 'Surely you don't intend to go off for tea just when Alison's dog is coming up for trial?'

'If I see just one more sheepdog go through his performances I shall scream,' Geralda said

215

crossly. 'I'm parched with thirst and my feet are killing me. If you won't take me, Keith, then I shall ask Toby.' Here she paused as though this ultimatum should make Keith instantly accompany her to the tea tent.

But far from that, not only did he not bother to reply, but Toby put in quickly, 'Do be patient just a little longer, Geralda. I wouldn't miss Alison's dog for worlds; it's not the sort of thing one sees every day of the week.'

At which Geralda swung angrily on her heel and marched off in the direction of the tea tent.

The others hardly noticed her departure. Hector, absorbed in his task, was standing in front, his back to the spectators, guiding Correy simply by whistles and signals, and as Alison saw her little dog crouch low on the grass, then race off to do his bidding, she was thinking how small he looked in comparison to the splendid dogs who had preceded him.

But she need not have been despondent. As he emerged over the brow of a little hill, driving three sheep before him, it was clear that he was giving an outstanding performance. He drove the sheep running in wide sweeps of half circles behind them, never nipping them, or barking, never hurrying them, yet at the same time preventing them straying away and getting scattered. Every whistle and signal of

216

Hector's he obeyed instantly, crouching in the grass or creeping forward gently behind the sheep, his ears cocked, listening intently, then darting forward to obey Hector's whistles.

Soon there was a little murmur of approval amongst the onlookers and Alison knew that she was not alone in her admiration for this gallant little dog. He seemed to have won all hearts, and when he finally guided the sheep into the fold, she knew that he had quite a following amongst the spectators.

When the trial was over Keith turned to Alison and began, 'Well, Alison, I take back all I said about that little mongrel of yours, I—'

He spoke warmly and enthusiastically and Alison could not repress a pang of annoyance when just then Geralda reappeared on the scene. Her hair had been carefully combed and her make-up restored.

'Don't tell me you're *still* here,' she queried incredulously. 'Why, I've seen the whole place from stem to stern on top of two cups of scalding tea and a cream cake made by a lady in a purple hat. I simply couldn't refuse it—although what it will do to my waistline I dread to think!'

Evidently her sojourn in the tea tent had restored all her vitality and she seemed disconcerted when Keith, instead of responding to her mood, continued his conversation with Alison. 'Yes, you did right to name him Pride of Abercorrey, because today he has brought fame to the house of Heseltine.'

He fell into step with Alison as they turned away and Geralda, with a moue of annoyance, moved off quickly with Toby; her voice, rather over-loud and too vivacious, carried back to Alison as Geralda plunged into conversation with him.

'You know, Alison, I'm sure Correy will win,' Keith was saying. 'Certainly he deserves to do so. He was the quickest and most intelligent, and I never saw such wide sweeps as those he made when bringing in the sheep. He has marvellous style, and that's sure to count for a lot. I have to admire your spunk. Everyone ran down that little animal of yours, but you had faith in him and it has paid off. But then you were always a determined little cuss. Remember the time I dared you to jump from the end of the—'

But what memory of their past days he had been about to bring up she was never to know, because at that moment Geralda, striding ahead with Toby and talking at the top of her voice, tripped over the guy-rope of a tent and fell to the ground in the soft grass.

Keith had turned his head to glance back towards the spot where the sheepdog trials were continuing and did not notice the incident. Toby moved forward quickly to

218

help Geralda to her feet 'Are you hurt?' he asked anxiously.

Alison overheard Geralda reply, 'Oh, don't fuss, Toby. It's nothing.'

She was just about to scramble to her feet when Keith looked around. 'Geralda!' he exclaimed, and hurried to her assistance.

To Alison's surprise she saw Geralda sink back to the ground weakly. 'My ankle—I'm afraid I've sprained it,' she murmured, lying back helplessly.

'Put your arm around my neck. Now, easy does it.' Gently Keith lifted her to her feet where she stood on one leg and gingerly touched the other foot to the ground and then winced as though with pain.

As Alison caught Toby's look of amazement she had difficulty in suppressing a giggle. Really, there was no limit to which Geralda would not go when she wanted to catch a man's interest and bind him to her side.

'I don't know how I'm to walk to the car,' Geralda was saying faintly, leaning against Keith and contriving to look pale and frail.

'We'd better get you home as soon as possible and send for a doctor,' Keith said decidedly.

'Oh, that won't be necessary,' Geralda said quickly. 'But perhaps you could just help me a little, because I feel certain I won't be able to walk a step by myself.'

219

Geralda had certainly succeeded in recapturing Keith's interest, Alison was thinking a little bitterly as with Toby she trailed along behind Keith who was carrying Geralda. She managed to recline artistically in his arms, one white hand hanging limply over his shoulder.

'Did you see what I saw?' Toby asked Alison, as one unable to believe the evidence of his own eyes. 'She was actually getting to her feet when he came along and then suddenly she discovered that she'd sprained her ankle. You know, Alison, I may as well admit it, I felt pretty rotten when she threw me over, but this performance of hers has made me realize just how lucky I was to escape.'

Arrived at the car Keith carefully placed Geralda in the front seat and then went around and took his place behind the wheel.

Geralda's eyes were wide and ingenuous. 'I'm so sorry,' she told Toby and Alison who were standing looking on rather helplessly. 'But don't let this spoil your day: you two must go off and enjoy yourselves and don't give a thought to poor little me. After all, it's only a tiny sprain, not worth bothering about.'

Just then, over the loudspeakers it was announced that Number Sixteen had won the sheepdog trials.

'So your dog won—as I told you it would,'

Keith leaned forward to congratulate Alison. 'Now be sure to go up for the cup. It's a whopping great one, I know.'

He drove off with Geralda and Alison remained to claim the cup which, as Keith had prophesied, was enormous and ornate. A jubilant Hector took Correy home with him and Toby and Alison followed by car.

She was seated beside him with the big cup on her knee as they drove towards Abercorrey and Toby said with a half-humorous quirk on his lips, 'Well, Alison, as you undoubtedly know, I've made several attempts to pop the question to you since I came here, but each has been unsuccessful. It seems as if there's a hoodoo on me. However, I'm now going to make another attempt. We can hardly be interrupted here—at least I hope not. Perhaps at last I'll get the chance of saying that if you'll only reconsider me and if you think we could make a fresh start I'd devote my life to making you happy.'

'No, Toby,' she said firmly. 'We mustn't think of it. It would never do.'

'So you don't forgive me?' he asked, a slight tone of surprise in his voice. 'I was so sure that you would; you're the only girl in the world who would be big enough to overlook what happened. But I suppose it was too much to ask of anyone.'

'It's not that, Toby,' she said gently. 'It's that I've come to the conclusion that it would never have done—not even from the beginning. We would never have been happy, because I realize now that I was never in love—' She stopped.

'You were never really in love with me,' he finished.

'I'm afraid not,' she told him.

'Possibly that's why you find it easy to forgive,' he told her, with what for him was unusual perspicacity. 'It would be different if it were this Keith fellow, wouldn't it? You're in love with him, aren't you? You've fallen for him since you came here.'

'I'm afraid I was always in love with him,' Alison said reflectively. 'But when I accepted you I didn't know it. In fact I've only realized it lately myself.'

'It's as I always thought about you, Alison. You're a one-man woman. There isn't a fickle inch in you, and if you're really in love with this fellow I know I don't stand a chance. I only hope, for your sake, that he's in love with—' he stopped, embarrassed.

'That he's in love with me! I don't even hope that—not now,' she told him. 'Not with Geralda as a rival!'

'I must say it struck me that she was making a strong play for him,' Toby admitted, 'and you must admit that when Geralda puts her mind to anything, she—'

'She always succeeds,' Alison finished.

'However, he may have more sense than I

222

had,' Toby put in, bitterness in his voice. 'Maybe he'll see through Geralda in good time and give her a wide berth.'

'There's no reason why he should,' Alison had to admit sadly, 'because, for once in her life, Geralda is in earnest. She's really in love with him.'

'Then there's no more to be said,' Toby told her. 'I only wish there could have been a different ending to my journey to Scotland. But no matter what you say I'll always think that if you hadn't come back here and met Keith Heseltine again there might have been a chance for me.'

When they stopped in front of the house he wryly studied her troubled face for a moment before kissing her gently on the forehead. 'Don't worry Alison, this is my cue for quietly disappearing from the scene. I only hope, my dear, that your *affaire du coeur* proves more successful than mine.'

CHAPTER ELEVEN

Alison slipped indoors for a moment and proudly placed the giant silver cup on a dark Jacobean table where it glowed against the sombre wood.

Then she hurried out again to join Hector at the stables and assist him to rub down

223

Correy, feed him and tuck him into his nest in the pen in the corner.

Hector regarded Correy admiringly as he curled up comfortably in the straw. 'Yon's a bonnie dog,' he pronounced with satisfaction, 'though it's not everyone sees his good points.'

'Oh, you mean Keith,' Alison smiled. 'I think Correy's performance has quite converted him. In fact, he told me he had brought fame to Abercorrey.'

'Did he now?' Hector sounded pleased. Then almost immediately his rugged features grew lugubrious. 'But I'll tell you someone who isnae over fond of poor Correy, and that's Miss Geralda.'

'Well, I suppose she isn't,' Alison conceded, 'but then she's not used to country life.'

'Maybe, but I doubt poor Correy will be long at Abercorrey if she gets her way.'

'What do you mean?' Alison asked, alarmed.

'What I say is, she's a bonnie lady, I'll no deny, but she's a fly one as well.'

'Fly?' Alison asked, puzzled.

'Aye, cute as a fox, and it's easy to see she has set her mind on Mr Keith. Well, like I say, if she gets him to the altar there'll be a gay lot of changes at Abercorrey, I'm thinking, and poor Correy will be the first to go, I can tell you that—and myself forby, no doubt,' he ended gloomily.

Alison felt her heart sink. Geralda's tactics must be very obvious for Hector to speak out in such a forthright manner.

'Or no, Keith wouldn't part with Correy now, he's much too proud of him.'

'Maybe! But a woman as bonnie as Miss Geralda would get her own way with a man if she set her mind to it. You mark my words, there'll be a good many changes about Abercorrey when she becomes the mistress.'

Alison gazed at him uncertainly: his words only confirmed her own worst conclusions as to Geralda's future intentions.

'Dinnae look so fashed, lassie,' Hector said, his craggy features breaking into a wide grin. 'I was near fit to burst my sides laughing the day. It was as good as a pantomine when she let on she'd hurst herself at the Gathering. I was watching her and she didn't as much as dint her wee finger when she fell. It was all put on so as to get Mr Keith by himself, though I was surprised he was took in by her, for a babe in arms could have seen through her.' Hector broke into a roar of laughter as he recollected the scene.

His amusement was infectious and, in spite of herself, Alison found herself giving an answering smile. Yes, Geralda had been pretty blatant in her efforts to secure Keith's undivided attention—so obvious in fact that even Hector, his mind already filled with the

225

heady knowledge that Correy stood a good chance of winning the cup, had noticed her. And for the first time, Alison wondered if indeed Keith had been taken in by the charade. She was a little ashamed to find herself hoping that he had seen through her ruse and with his usual devilish perversity had been only simulating concern when he had carried her back to the car.

A glance in the mirror in her own room showed Alison that a day at the Gathering had not been the best thing in the world for her appearance. She took a hot bath, then dressed for dinner and brushed up her dark hair until it formed a halo around her small, pale face.

She must take a peep at the cup again before dinner, she decided. She went downstairs again and stood before the table feeling a renewed thrill of achievement. Then, satisfied, she drifted towards a cosy corner near the giant chimneyplace. Here she ensconced herself in the chair that was always used by Seaton on his rare appearances downstairs. It was a tall straight-backed chair with old-fashioned wings which made a cosy nook against the draughts that occasionally swept through the hall. She felt safe in appropriating this chair because she felt sure that if Jennie had her way she would encourage him to stay in his room instead of coming down to dinner.

Once seated, she was too lazy to rise again

to fetch a magazine from the great wooden rack in which they were stored, or even to switch on the tall reading lamp which stood nearby. She gazed into the fire in drowsy satisfaction, feeling her eyelids closing and making no attempt to fight the languor that seemed to steal upon her. Geralda had been right, she thought sleepily: it had been a tiring day—wonderful as it had been as far as she was concerned.

She awoke to hear Keith saying, 'I suppose we should be grateful you didn't turn up in that outfit for the Gathering!'

He was standing near a sofa on which Geralda reclined gracefully in an elaborate dress of diaphanous rust-coloured silk: the shade which was wonderfully becoming and dramatic against her blonde beauty seemed to emphasise her almond-shaped eyes.

'Not that I've the smallest complaint,' Keith went on, 'because you look very lovely indeed!'

'You really mean that?' Geralda asked eagerly.

'Yes, I think you're the most beautiful woman I've ever seen,' he told her slowly.

It was only too apparent that they did not know that she was there and Alison found herself in a quandary. Perhaps the dinner-gong would sound in a moment or two and in the general exodus towards the dining-room she would be able to slip from her hiding-place unnoticed.

'I put this dress on especially for you,' Geralda told him, her voice sultry. 'I knew I must have looked perfectly ghastly this afternoon.'

'Well, I can say in all honesty that you look anything but ghastly now!'

'And is that all you have to say?' Geralda's voice was coaxing and her long slender arms were reaching up to his shoulders where he stood close behind her. 'Just that I am very beautiful? Nothing else?'

'What else would you like me to say?' he asked. 'Surely that should be sufficient for any woman! Do you not know me well enough yet to know that I am not a man who is good at saying sweet nothings?'

'It's not enough for me, darling. Not by a long chalk.' Geralda's voice was low and tense. 'Can't you guess what I want you to say?'

Keith was gazing down at her, his dark face enigmatic. 'I'm afraid I haven't the remotest idea, my dear Geralda.'

Geralda pouted. 'Don't pretend to be so dense. You're like all men: you want me to spell it out, so your ego will be satisfied. All right, I'll say it. I love you, Keith: you're the only man in the world whom I could really care for. Now are you satisfied?'

There was a short pause, then Keith said levelly, 'Far from being satisfied, completely bewildered. I can't imagine what a woman of the world like yourself could see in me, an uncouth Highlander.'

'Perhaps that's what attracts me to you,' she countered. 'I'm sick of sleek, glib men who always have the right answers. You're so completely different, Keith! I'm not surprised that you and Alison were keen on each other when you were boy and girl, but now that she's engaged to David surely that's all in the past.'

'But she's not engaged to David,' he told her.

Geralda's slender arms slid from his shoulders. 'What on earth do you mean? Of course she's engaged: Hester heard it all.'

'It's obvious you're not *au fait* with present developments. I used some strong-arm methods with Hester and got some interesting results. As you may have heard, she's an inveterate little liar, but I wrung the truth out of her. It seems that, very far from accepting David, Alison turned him down very emphatically indeed.'

'I see,' Geralda said tightly after a few seconds. 'So I've been making a fool of myself; flinging myself at your head. Well, you ought to be satisfied!'

'Let's say that you were never cut out for life in the wilds of Scotland.'

'Don't try to put me off,' Geralda snapped. 'I suppose you find Alison perfectly "cut out", as you call it, for the role of wife to the laird of Correybrae?'

'Yes, that amongst other things.'

'I see. So suitability to life at Correybrae and the capacity to endure those ghastly country events is the criterion by which you choose a future wife!' she exclaimed angrily, throwing discretion to the winds.

'Not altogether! It just so happens that I love her.'

In the silence that followed this statement Alison felt her heart beat almost suffocatingly as joy raced through her in great waves. She pulled herself further back in the armchair, loath to be discovered, and for a moment she wondered wildly if they could hear the thudding of her heart.

'Suppose Alison doesn't see herself in that role?' Geralda sounded bitter and frustrated.

'I know I stand every chance of being turned down,' he told her. 'Alison has heard too many horrible stories about me, perhaps, to make her willing to risk giving her life into my hands. However, I'm going to risk it anyway.'

'And do you think I'm going to hang around waiting for the outcome? Do you seriously imagine that should Alison refuse you I shall be waiting here for you to offer yourself to me as second best? I'm not the sort of woman who's ready to take any other woman's cast-offs. I'm leaving!'

As she spoke Geralda got up from the sofa and with surprising alacrity for one with an injured ankle swung from the hall. Alison could hear the soft thud of her feet as she ran up the carpeted stairs.

'My, my, but you've made a remarkably quick recovery!' Keith called after her, and his voice held mockery.

For a moment Geralda turned and hesitated. She seemed on the point of an acid retort. Then as though realizing that she had hopelessly betrayed herself she turned and marched defiantly up the remainder of the stairs.

Shortly afterwards the dinner-gong sounded and when Keith had gone towards the dining-room with Morag, Alison slid from her place in the shady corner and joined Hester as she came downstairs.

'Where's everyone?' Hester asked, looking around the table as they took their places.

'Well, Toby has gone off. Some urgent business has arisen in London which must be seen to immediately,' Keith told her very seriously. 'He's flying back tonight.'

'Why in such a hurry? I rather liked him, and goodness knows we don't have visitors so often,' Hester said petulantly.

'Seaton's resting after our trip to Aberdeen,' Morag said, as though to divert Hester's attention, and Alison wondered if she knew the reason for Toby's hurried departure. She had learned that Morag had much more perspicacity than she had given her credit for at first acquaintance.

'I'm so glad Seaton is resting,' Morag went on. 'He has had quite enough excitement for one day—although I think the trip has done him good. We're going to do much more of this sort of thing in future. Poor Geralda has a headache and is having a tray to her room. I'm sure the Gathering was too much for her. She's not used to these open-air events. I'm sorry I missed Correy's trials,' she went on, turning to Alison. 'I'd have loved to have been there, but of course this outing with Seaton had to take priority. However, I most sincerely congratulate you. I expect Hector's delighted with himself.'

'Actually it was Hector who made it possible. I feel rather a hypocrite taking all the credit.'

As Alison thanked Morag she was dimly aware that there was something different about her this evening: for one thing, this had been a long speech from Morag, who usually limited herself to a few awkward words in a vain effort to smooth over the nasty patches that were only too frequent at the Heseltine table. Then it struck Alison that Morag was very well satisfied about the trip into Aberdeen with Seaton: it meant that she had spent the entire day in her husband's company—a rare treat for her—and suddenly

232

it struck Alison that Morag was deeply in love with her rather elderly and invalid husband, and for the first time she wondered what exactly had taken place to give Morag this new air of happiness. She had spoken with an air of authority and without the touch of apology that had been part and parcel of her manner.

'You should have been at the Gathering.' Keith began to twit Hester in the almost indolent way that was customary. 'David was there and you would have had the opportunity of having a chat with him. How was it that you were able to stay away?'

'You can cut it out, Keith,' Hester told him shortly. 'I'm not going to waste my time on David any longer. I realize I've been behaving like a silly lovesick teenager. I'm leaving here as soon as I can, and as far as I'm concerned the sooner the better.'

There was a silence after this and Alison thought she saw a shade of embarrassment cross Keith's face and she wondered for a moment if he regretted his idle teasing. 'You're not leaving because nasty Keith says horrid things, are you?' he asked, toying with his soup spoon.

'Hester is leaving because she wants to,' Morag said with such a new air of authority that every eye at the table immediately turned to her. 'We had a heart-to-heart chat this afternoon while Seaton was gossiping with some old cronies of his he spotted when we were driving along Castle Street and Hester was telling me that she plans to go to London and study dress-designing. She realizes now that it's the sort of life she has always wanted, and I for one heartily approve if her happiness lies in that direction.'

There was another silence after this rather surprising speech from Morag. Then Keith said softly, 'Don't tell me, Morag, that at last you've taken a strong line with this little hussy?'

'There was no question of "taking a strong line", as you call it,' Morag said firmly. 'It's simply that I think it's an excellent idea.'

'I *want* to go away,' Hester told him fiercely. 'I'm fed up with Abercorrey and everything to do with it. Morag's right, dress-designing is the only kind of life I really want.'

'And you're helping her towards her ambition?' Keith remarked to Morag.

'Yes, I've promised to ask Seaton at the first propitious moment to give his consent—and to endow the project,' Morag said calmly. 'You see, this afternoon both of us did something we should have done some time ago—we faced up to the fact that we're not really compatible persons. One of us had to go, and clearly it had to be—'

'Me,' Hester finished. 'And now it's happened I'm glad. I only wish we'd brought things to a head ages ago.'

'I suppose we both shrank from unpleasantness,' her stepmother said thoughtfully. 'I know I did. But eventually I had to come to terms with the realities of the situation.'

'Congratulations,' Keith told her. 'I've been wondering when you'd buckle down to the job. But to tell the truth,' he turned to his sister, 'I'll miss you when you're gone. I'll have no one to fight with and keep me on my toes.'

'Don't worry, you'll soon find someone to take that place,' Hester told him, her eyes going to Alison.

'I hope so. Otherwise I'll begin to find life dull too.'

As he said this, Alison was acutely aware of the words she had overheard in the hall. 'I know I stand every chance of being turned down—however, I'm going to risk it,' and she hoped that the happy flush that rose to her cheeks would go unnoticed.

'Yes, I hope I shall soon find someone to fight with,' Keith was saying slowly. 'Someone who will put me in my place and keep me in order, for I admit I like spirited people. I like a girl with plenty of spunk and get-up-and-go. I don't think I should mind losing every fight to such a one.'

As they rose from table Alison knew that he would propose soon—it was not in his nature to put things off once he had made up his mind—and she was acutely aware that she did not know what answer she would give him. She loved him, she knew, but could she trust him? The Keith she had come home to was a very different person from the boy she had once loved. He was the man who had grown up bitter and twisted with the knowledge that his reckless challenge to his brother had been the cause of his death. Could a man who had let jealousy of his elder brother carry him to such lengths be a good husband? And suddenly all her happiness was dissolved and she knew that, much as she loved him, she dreaded the quandary his proposal would place her in.

She made an excuse to go up early, glad to feel that she would have the night in which to think things over and to try to straighten out her thoughts.

She was approaching the door of Seaton's room when Morag and Jennie came out. Jennie's cheeks were flushed and for once her habitual sly grin had disappeared.

They paused in the middle of the corridor and Alison, hesitating a moment about brushing past, was surprised to hear Morag say in a clear, firm voice, 'In future I and I alone shall say when my husband is to keep to his room and when he is to join us at dinner; nor will I permit you to sadden him any longer by your perpetual stories about Ian.

You've already too much power in this house, and in future you will have no further say where my husband's welfare is concerned.'

'And why shouldn't I have power in this house?' Jennie seemed momentarily surprised, then went on recklessly, 'It's my right and due.'

'What exactly do you mean by that?' Morag asked icily.

'I'm entitled to a place in this house.' Jennie's voice had risen and her accent had broadened. 'Oh, everyone thinks that Flora Heseltine had her stroke because she was watching from her window and saw Ian drowned. But it was far different. It was snobbery that killed her. I've as much right in this house as you have, because I was everything but wife in name to Ian, and he promised me he'd marry me. He loved me—me, who was only a maid in the house—and would have defied his parents to marry me, he was that much in love. But Flora wouldn't have it. When she knew what we had in mind to do, it was too much for her, and she fell down with a stroke, killed by her own wicked pride. But he would have married me all the same: I know that, if that Keith hadn't murdered him. So you needn't put on any of your airs with me, my fine madam!'

'How dare you say such things!' Morag had lowered her voice, but it carried clearly to

237

Alison as the two women ignored her presence. 'What would become of my husband if he were to hear of this?'

'He won't hear of it unless you tell him.' Jennie flung back her head defiantly. 'And I doubt you will, keen as you are to get me out! Oh no, you'll not get rid of me that easy. By right my place is here and here I intend to stay.' Jennie glared at her mistress, resolute and defiant.

'But that's where you're wrong, Jennie,' Morag said firmly. 'For a long time I've allowed you too much ascendancy in this household. You've brazenly usurped my position and I weakly allowed you to. But all that's coming to an end. Unless you change your attitude I'll see that you leave Abercorrey, even if it means my husband must learn of your association with Ian. No doubt you were counting on the fact that I'd hesitate to pain him by telling the whole facts of Flora's death and Ian's association with you, but I've decided, loath as I am to do it, to ensure that never again will I be treated like a nonentity under my own roof.'

It was at that instant that the door of Seaton's room was pushed wide and Alison realized that it had been slightly ajar during Morag's altercation with Jennie.

In the doorway appeared Seaton, pallid and worn, dressd in an old checked dressing-gown. In the deathly silence that greeted his arrival his soft faint voice was clearly heard, and somehow its quiet tones made the impact of his words more dramatic than if he had shouted. 'I've heard what you said, Jennie. So you think that because I have shown unpardonable weakness as far as you're concerned I'm prepared to condone your behaviour. So it was you who was encouraging my son in his vices—here under my roof! Not only that, but since his death, you have systematically poisoned my mind against my younger son because you blame him for Ian's death and see him as stealing from you the place that you think would have been yours. But believe me, you would never have been Ian's wife—not if I could prevent it! And not out of snobbery, as you flatter yourself, but because we wanted a very different type of wife for our son. You are a wicked woman, and my only regret is that through my love for Ian I allowed you to gain such control in this house. But your reign has come to an end. From now on you'll do as my wife says, or leave Abercorrey.'

'You can't mean that, not after all this time,' Jennie protested. She had turned white. For a moment she gazed at him in disbelief, then realizing that he was adamant, turned with pallid face and disappeared along the corridor.

He turned to Morag. 'Can you forgive me, my dear?' he asked brokenly.

'Seaton dear!' Morag's eyes glowed, then filled with happy tears that needed no interpretation.

*   *   *

Later that night Alison stood for a long time at that corner window in her room looking out over the scene on which Flora must so often have gazed: darkness veiled the countryside with its awesome panorama of moor and mountain, but the sound of the river was loud—and would grow more noisy as winter settled in.

The drowning of Ian in that dangerous spot had been the beginning of Keith's tragedy, she realized, and in it was rooted all his bitterness, but at least he need not carry the added burden of believing that he was also the cause of the stroke which had struck his mother down and from which she had never recovered. It had been assumed that she had witnessed the drowning, whereas in fact it had been her interview with Jennie that had caused it.

Alison could imagine that scene: Jennie fearful and defiant, claiming her position as Ian's wife in all but name. She had counted on the blind devotion his parents had for their elder son, their yielding to every whim of his, to carry her to the position she coveted, that of mistress of Abercorrey, as Ian's wife.

240

Flora's stroke had put paid to that idea, and almost immediately Ian's death had followed. A bitter hatred for Keith had grown in her heart and she had fed poison to Seaton in her never-ending criticisms of him.

Before she got into bed that night Alison resolved that she would relate to Keith what she had overheard first thing in the morning. Perhaps knowing the truth would help to heal the dreadful mental wound he had received and make him more like the boy she had known so long ago.

On the following morning the little maid who brought Alison her early morning cup of tea had an exciting news item to recount. 'would you credit it, Miss Conrad left, without as much as saying goodbye to anyone! When I went into her room it was empty and her things were gone, and Sandy says he saw her big white car pass the gates of the lodge first thing this morning.'

But Alison suspected that the girl was well aware of the reason for Geralda's departure. There was very little could be hidden from the servants at Abercorrey, she had discovered.

So Geralda had departed, Alison was thinking as she leaned back against her pillows and sipped her tea. She had made her play for Keith and had failed, and now she was on her way—to pastures new, no doubt. It was not in Geralda's nature to repine:

Keith might have been the one great love of her life, but she would make do with second best when she found a suitable man. Was it possible that she and Toby would take up together again? Stranger things had happened!

It was at this point in her thoughts that there was a tap on her door and when she called out, 'Come in,' to her surprise Keith appeared in the doorway.

'Well, may I come in?' he asked.

'You've grown very polite, all of a sudden,' Alison told him. 'Last time you called, you didn't even bother to knock, if I remember rightly.'

'Ah, but this time I'm a suppliant,' he told her, 'and must mind my ps and qs.'

He came into her room and closed the door and as he crossed the carpet he said, 'Mind you, I didn't think you'd still be in bed. You're turning into a right lazybones, more fitted for life in Paris than in the Highlands where we're all up by cockcrow and out and about.'

He was silent for a moment, then said, 'I don't know if you've already heard, but Geralda left early this morning. She has grown bored with us, I think, and wanted to continue her Highland tour.'

'Very probably,' Alison agreed gravely.

'But I've been up and about myself for hours,' he went on, 'and a lonely time I've been having of it. I miss the long-legged girl who used to "run about the braes" with me and 'pu the gowans fine".'

'And is that what you've come in to tell me?' Alison asked. 'It's as well you did, however, because there's something I feel you ought to know—although I hardly know how to begin.'

He was silent, watching her troubled face intently.

'Yesterday evening I overheard a conversation between Morag and Jennie—or rather I was present, but they were so preoccupied that they paid no attention to me. Jennie apparently had been insolent to Morag just once too often and Morag tackled her about it, and when she did so, Jennie said—She said that that she had as much right to be here as Morag herself, because—well, because she and Ian had been lovers and—'

'And he had promised to marry her,' he ended.

'So you knew?'

'Of course I knew: do you think such a thing could go on in this house without my discovering it eventually? Besides, neither of them made any very serious attempt to cover it up. Ian was bored and Jennie was very pretty in those days, as you probably remember. The affair was a diversion for him—nothing more. You know what he was like.'

'You mean he didn't seriously intend to marry her?'

'Of course not! It was just a gambit to win her. Ian was simply wearing out the days until he would be twenty-one and would be able to get away from here with the part of his inheritance that would come to him on his coming of age. Jennie would have very soon found herself abandoned as soon as the money was under his control.'

'Perhaps Jennie knew—or guessed—' Alison went on, 'because it seems she forced an interview on your mother. This was on the day Ian was drowned, you understand—and told her that she and Ian were to be married. It was than that your mother had her stroke—'

'It was then? Not later, when—' His voice was no more than a whisper. He caught her hand and squeezed it. 'Those are the most wonderful words I think I've ever heard, Alison. So it was not my fault that—'

'No, it happened previously to Ian's accident. You need not blame yourself any more.'

Now he was pacing up and down the room with long strides. 'Not having to reproach myself any more. How wonderful that is! The thought has haunted me, made me miserable night and day, year after year—the thought that I was to blame for that fatal stroke!'

As he spoke he stopped and stared through that corner window at the scene where the boulder blocked the main current of the river and threw up a great burst of spray.

'It was just about this time of the year that Ian died,' he reminded her. 'And, do you know, I wasn't entirely to blame for that either.'

'No?' Alison held her breath, willing him to go on.

'No, Jennie was there. Her manner was strange and feverish, I remember. She had just come from my mother's room, I realize that now. She wanted to talk to Ian right away, tell him of what she had done. Wanted to concoct a story with him that would sound convincing—because at that time she could not have known than my mother would never be able to tell the story herself. But there I was with Ian. As Jennie came along he boasted that he could dive into the pool at that time of the year. At first I warned him, but Jennie—I suppose it was because she was in the habit of flattering him, but also because I truly think she didn't realize the danger—said "If anyone can do it you can, Ian," or something to that effect, and of course, after that there was no stopping him. It was then I joined in too. "Oh yes, there's no one like you at diving," I said jeeringly. I don't remember the exact words, but certainly when I saw he was determined to

245

show off I didn't dissuade him, although I thought it was a foolhardy thing to do. Afterwards Jennie didn't own up to her own part in it, but spread the story that I had dared him when the river was in full spate.

'All I can say now in self-defence is that when he dived and stayed down I dived after him, getting this—' As he spoke he pointed to the great scar that marred the line of his broad temple. 'I was never a good diver, as you know, but a strong swimmer, but he was swept away in that turbulent water before I could save him. Hester had come on the scene and when she saw him snatched from my hands and borne away she had no mercy on me. She ran off to the house and spread the story that I had dared him, because no one would believe that any sensible person would have attempted the dive at that time of the year.'

There was a long silence when he had finished and Alison said, 'But why didn't you defend yourself? Why have you let this story go on until now?'

'What would have been the use?' he asked. 'Had I tried to defend myself I should have had to mention Jennie's part in the tragedy. I knew what had been going on, remember, and I was fearful that the smallest hint might mean that the whole sordid story would break upon my father—at the very time when he was least able to bear any additional sorrow.

All I could do for him was to leave him with the idea that Ian had been an ideal character. It's been all that has held him on to life all these years. Until now, when I truly believe that at last he is strong enough to bear it.'

He had seated himself beside her bed once more and now she touched that scar on his temple gently with her fingertip. 'I'm so sorry, Keith,' she whispered. 'I didn't know.'

But she was thinking that the boy she had known had not changed so radically. She should have known that he would not have done a mean and cowardly thing like tempting his brother into the turbulent river while he himself remained in safety. That scar had been the price he had paid when he had risked his own life to save the reckless, vain young man that Ian had been.

'Tell me,' he asked abruptly in the silence, 'why did you turn David down?'

'Oh, I—I—' She fumbled for words. 'I don't quite know.'

'You don't lke him?'

'On the contrary, I like him immensely,' she said rather smugly.

'Then why don't you marry him?' he demanded.

'Oh, it's just that, nice as he is, he isn't the man for me.'

'Would I do, then?' he asked abruptly.

As Alison nodded silently she could hardly repress a smile. How like him to express a proposal in such a way, she was thinking as she was folded in his arms.

Later he drew from his pocket something that gleamed dully yellow-brown in the light from the sombre sky. A bracelet of cairngorms fastened with a silver chain. 'This will have to do until we can get an engagement ring,' he told her as he fastened it on her wrist. 'By the way, what are your favourite jewels? To think I don't even know!'

For an instant there flashed through Alison's mind the time she had been asked that question by Toby. She had told him that aquamarines were her favourites and he had instantly rejected the idea. It would be different with Keith, she knew.

And it was. 'Aquamarines are my favourite stones—after cairngorms, of course,' she said demurely.

'Then that is what you shall have,' he said in that abrupt manner that was typical of him.

And Alison, hearing that sharp decisive answer, felt her heart overflow: at last she had found the only man for her; the only man in the world who could bring her happiness. It had been a sort of test and he had measured up to it—as she knew he would measure up to all the tests in their life together.